L. N. WHITE

The Hunted

Contents

0. The Beginning of Cleo Knightley

We always sit at the three-tiered fountain at night. I looked at the water and saw the full moon reflecting. There was something different about me; I didn't have my usual hazel eyes. They were bright red, like the eyes of a pureblood vampire. It made me gasp. My brown hair was slowly turning amber. Suddenly, the water turned into blood. "Ezra..." was all I could manage before my throat burned. More blood came out of my cough. As soon as I started feeling pain, I started crying. The insides of my body were burning. As my heart and lungs squeezed, I felt dizzy. Part of me didn't want to be human anymore; it just wanted to be natural again.

"Cleo, I do not want to pressure you, but please." Ezra pleaded with me. Being my soulmate, I knew he wanted the best for me. He hated seeing me in pain. Those blood pills he dumped in his hand caught my eye. I knew I should release this beast that was inside of me.

However, I didn't want to.

I refused.

Taking the pills, I scooped them into my hand. I have no idea how many there were. I used the water bottle that we had brought with us. I couldn't hold down the water; it tasted horrible.

I felt like I was going to die. Something cut my tongue, and I felt a sharp pain in my mouth. There was an ache for something, water?

That's not what it was.

I don't want to change; it's not time yet. I knew what was happening but didn't want it to happen.

But I was also in a lot of pain. My blood and whatever was left in my stomach were coming out. It hurt to move and keep my eyes open, but I wanted to get away from Ezra.

It was time to give in, so I grabbed and bit Ezra's arm. His blood filled my mouth and soothed my burning throat. I took whatever he offered. When he pulled away, I tried to fight for more. Shaking his head, he said, "No. It's time to end your mortal life." He grabbed my head to tilt it back and bit my neck.

I felt the coolness of his venom start from my neck and slowly relieve my burning body. I felt a chill run down my spine as he pulled me closer, taking more and more. I finally opened my eyes all the way and saw the moon. The moon was full. It's starting its life, like I was—a new beginning. My life is about to change. Things were about to change for me and everyone as I am the last known member of the Knight family.

I could feel my insides twist and turn, and my heartbeat slowed.

There was a knock on my door; I knew who it was. As I opened the door, I smiled, "Ezra." Ezra gave me a weak smile. He stood by the desk when he came in. I touched his upper arm, and he seemed tense. "What's up, Ezra?" I asked.

I double-checked with Hardin to make sure it wasn't a mistake, but it wasn't." He said.

"Ezra, you're freaking me out. Please don't tell me it's Mortimer or Kolby." My voice trailed off.

"They are still imprisoned at the Fae Court. But somehow Natalia will get Mortimer out." Ezra paused again. "And will send him back in time."

"I am not understanding. How can you be certain Mortimer was sent to the past if he is still in prison?" I questioned.

He paused and said, "You have an aunt who was like a mentor to me at one point in my life before the second Kolby attack and the death of your family. Estrid is her name. She has a message for you from your parents." Ezra got up and walked towards the door, and opened it. There was a woman who resembled a Viking goddess.

It was the fledgling that warned my family. She smiled softly and said, "Hello, Princess Cleo."

1. Aisling

"Selene." he exclaimed with awe. I could not see him in the bright light as he entered it. To cover my eyes, I used my left arm to block the light. As I squinted, I was able to see him better. All I saw was the back of his head; his hair was the same colour as mine.

Dad?

As I approached, I began to walk closer. An ethereal purple light shone in the sky as the man reached out to it.

A soft voice said, "Accept this gift, and you will be damned for the rest of your life. You will never know rest." The man continued to reach for the gift. In a flash, the man had disappeared. Suddenly, a woman appeared with grey eyes and light lavender hair. There was a smile on her face, which revealed her fangs. Selena, the Goddess responsible for the creation of vampires. "Do what you must to free us, Princess." She said, but her mouth wasn't moving. She points behind me to Ezra in the middle of the lake. I was unable to run towards him when I tried to do so.

"Cleo…" I heard the man say. When I turned to look behind me, I could no longer see anything. "You are the true pureblood princess." Hearing him became increasingly difficult, "You- protect the people- Valentines- back. The next- to rule- Cleo!"

I gasped and awoke from my sleep. I placed my hand over my head as I was dripping with sweat. As I looked around, it was still late at night. Since I became pureblood again, I have had the same dream. It was difficult for me to identify the voice. After getting out of bed, I went to the bathroom. After splashing ice water on my face, I dried it off. It was strange to see my old face in the mirror. My mortal one had become so familiar to me.

I returned to my bed. I was drawn to the letter I had initially believed to be from an unknown sender. However, it turned out to be my older brother, Cassius Knightley. There is nothing I look forward to more than seeing him again. I have not forgotten about that letter.

My brother's letter was tightly held in my hand. Since I have a high probability of losing control, I cannot go back and check if he is still at that school. I began to mess with my choker necklace. It was something I always wore as a child. The choker was made of ashy blue ribbon and a gold metal piece shaped like a crow with dark blue gems for eyes. Throughout the generations, it has been passed down to the women in the family, beginning with my great-grandmother.

"Are you paying attention?" Hardin snapped.

My head snapped towards him; I was staring into the fire, oblivious to the conversation taking place. The fire made the pale pink in his hair appear less prominent as I looked at the boy.

"I apologise, but no." I replied.

"The plan involves you and Ezra not messing up the timeline. Make sure you're paying attention so you don't fuck it up. One small mistake can ruin everything you know as true. Especially because Morgana is watching secretly over Kat, so she can't go with you two." Hardin sighed and sat down. Next to Miri, he sat. Even though this meeting was intended for the royalty that attends the school. There was a lower-ranking Fae noble present, Miri.

Hardin was right, I needed to pay attention. Morgana won't be there to help me, she normally helps my mum with whatever she needs. But she did spend some time with me when I was a child.

Sure I'll have Ezra but neither of us had ever been alive during that time. It's just the 90s so it should not be any different than now. Morgana was not at Cypress during the time that we needed, so it would have been perfect to have her with us.

There was also the headmaster and Renee present. Since Renee is the one who casts the spell and the headmaster because we are still his students. As well as The Viking Princess, although she is not a princess. But she indeed appeared and acted like a member of the royal family. In addition, she has been around for a long enough time that no one questions her legitimacy. Mainly since she is a member of the original vampire family, the Knights.

Miri put her arm through Hardin's when I realised why she was here. Despite appearing to want to pull away, he did not do so. His mother, the fae Queen, wishes to continue the bloodline. He must be with her for that reason. The last I heard, Hardin was dating Michael, the shifter Prince. Michael sat in a way that would not allow him to see Hardin or Miri.

Ezra's hand touched mine; I was unaware he was still sitting beside me. We were seated in a lounge chair. I smiled at him as I brushed the dark curls from his face. Since becoming a pureblood again, he has been a great help. I am grateful for his gentleness with me. "He means well. Hardin is stressed." A smile spread across Ezra's face as he looked at me. "You must know what to expect during that time."

Nodding, I placed the letter on my lap and held his hand tightly. I hesitated to commit to anything serious until I learned that Freyja, Ezra's ex, had moved on. There is still no communication between us. I don't blame her. I took someone from her.

My eyes were fixed on the ground. A red carpet was adorned with gold designs. The school had carpets in several rooms. It was my mum's favourite colour combination. She used to say that it reminded her of her own life. The colour of her human life is gold, and the colour of her vampire life is red. It is clear to me what she means; I was so eager to understand what she meant as a child.

"Princess, you need to pay attention. You could lose everything you know if you disrupt the timeline. You must take the pages that explain who Mortimer is connected to. Find him and bring him to the present." The Viking Princess, Estrid, instructed. She wore a light blue tunic with soft tan leggings to match her long dirty blonde hair in Viking braids. I would have thought she was from the past if I did not know better. After all, she was around when I was growing up, so I know better than that. She would tell me bedtime stories of the adventures she used to have before she was turned, but I can barely recall them.

I nodded in agreement. Eventually, Estrid must have noticed the letter.

"We will locate your brother, Princess, but for now, we must remain focused on the mission." Estrid said.

Renee cleared her throat. Estrid's formal manner makes her uncomfortable since she is not used to it. It's written all over her body. "We should test the spell first to see if it works."

Estrid waved the idea before explaining, "You need not worry, youngling. The Fae has used that spell many times before."

Renee started to say, "Yes, but I never-"

"Are you not the heir of Celine?" Estrid inquired, raising her eyebrows. As Renee was about to speak, Estrid interrupted her, "Then it should be no problem for you!"

She sighed heavily.

Light Matter Magick users are the only ones who can use the spell. It would have been my Fae sister, from my mortal life, and Renee to ensure that nothing happened to me. However, my sister, Katie, is still looking for a way to bring her mate back to her. As much as I would like to be able to assist her, I am unable to do so. I was trapped in a bracelet when she left, which unintentionally accelerated the human spell that was used against me. It has been renamed the hourglass spell since, while trapped, time accelerates, even just a little.

It was not a good idea to go back in time. Being a pureblood worsens matters, as I have no control over my power. I wish

Estrid had not remembered seeing Ezra and me in the past.

A silence fell over the room. "I think that's a good idea, Renee." Headmaster Grey stated.

Seeing the way Renee was flustered. "Yes, that is smart." I added.

Jon, the Hunter Prince, scoffed, "What is your issue?"

Looking into his eyes, I could not see any whites, only blacks. He looked like one of those black-eyed children in the urban legend. "There is a lot to take in, and being a vampire again is strange. I thought since I was a vampire, I would not have to deal with Mortimer again."

Hunters were not taken seriously enough when I was a child to be considered royalty or pureblood. Neither queens nor kings were permitted, let alone princes. In addition, I discovered that their leader is male. It is weird, and I am surprised that the council allowed this to pass. This prince is named after his father, Jon Jackson.

He raised an eyebrow at me and asked, "Why would you think that? You have a direct connection to that monster until the end of your life. It's your duty now to stop him."

"Why me?" I asked. "Why not Renee, since she is an heir? She has a direct bloodline to Celine, even if it is through Celine's sister or you since you and Mortimer are Tribloods. Would it not be possible for you to stop him? It has not yet been possible for me to mourn for my family. It may have happened to everyone years ago, but it has not been too long for me, the vampire me." He glanced away. "That's what I thought." I murmured.

As he looked at me with sympathy, he said, "Cleo." His dark eyes were looking deeply into my soul. "Let's take a break." He said to the room; he got up and extended his hand for me to take.

2. Ezra Grimwald

The two of us walked out of the room. After leaving that room, I felt a little better. In a whisper, I said, "I meant what I said."

"I get it. I wish there was a way around this so you didn't have to deal with it. Then you can mourn your family." Ezra said, "What if we take the day off? We go into town or whatever you want?"

"It's strange not being under room arrest." I chuckled. While blinking, I struggled to hold back tears as I explained, "It was also strange to have two people inside my head." Back then, I believed that I could return to my human form. Return to a much simpler life. "Everything seems chaotic now. I wish to help, but I also feel helpless." Trying to hold back tears was becoming increasingly difficult.

I was surprised by how wonderful Ezra smelt when he hugged me. My vampire scent must be responsible for this. I returned the hug. "Everything will be okay; I understand how overwhelmed you are." He said, his face buried in my hair.

I took another deep breath and said, "You smell excellent. I don't remember you smelling like this."

A soft chuckle escaped Ezra's lips. You must have been too busy to notice. Even without the Hourglass Spell, you have been busy these last few weeks." He pulled away. "Why don't we go into town?"

With a nod, I responded, "Sure. But why?"

He smiled as he said, "There was a place created specifically for you when you were younger. Now it is mainly for purebloods."

The other purebloods had already taken over after I was absent for a few years." I scoffed. "Don't they know my brother is still alive?"

"Everyone thought your whole family had died," he said as he shook his head. "That's what Kolby told everyone. Once I saw your brother at school, I knew he was alive. He went to school with my sister, after all. But if I knew you were the princess, I might have-" He sighed.

There was still a sense of unrest in Ezra about not being allowed to finish Kolby for his actions against me and my family. Nonetheless, I have always wondered if it was not me who stopped Ezra. Who did? "Who stopped you?"

As Ezra tilted his head to the side, he asked, "What do you mean?"

Looking down, I reflected, "When the Hourglass Spell trapped me, I saw that you had almost killed Kolby. If it wasn't me, then who was it?" I glanced back up, "I would like to thank them for saving you from making a serious mistake when I could not."

"Who told you I almost killed Kolby?"

I shrugged and replied, "I do not believe anyone did. I was the one who stopped you when I was trapped in the bracelet."

He paused briefly before revealing, "It was Hardin and his guards. They removed me before I could end Kolby."

"So, Hardin came with the guards?" I asked. The bracelet

was still pretty close to what took place."

It may be related to your psychic ability as a pureblood vampire. Since your father was an original, I can't even imagine how strong your abilities became." Ezra answered, "That would make sense."

"Yes, that would make sense." I paused, "Do you think you could take me home rather than go into town? I want to see my mum and see if my brother is still there."

He replied, "Sure. We'll need Renee or Hardin to make a portal, though." The majority of supernaturals have the ability to create short-range portals, but it was only the Fae who were able to create long-range portals.

We returned to the room we had left and overheard the headmaster talking to Hardin, Michael, and Jon. "It is tough for me to tell Cleo and Renee, but the deaths of the students began after Kolby and Mortimer escaped the Fae Court."

Suddenly, I felt as if my heart was being stabbed. No matter how strong I think I am, I cannot escape this weight. It has become too heavy for me to carry. They may be at the school at this very moment. A week of torture and torment was inflicted upon us by them. My family almost came to an end as a result of Kolby's actions. As my hand tightened into a fist, I felt my heart race.

I realised something was wrong when I heard someone yelp in pain and then a loud thud.

3. Vedriti

"Cleo!" Ezra shook me violently. There was an air of panic in his voice. It took me a moment to focus on him.

"Did you know about this?" I whispered to Ezra, struggling to find my voice. To even find myself in the mess that is currently taking place in my mind. By grasping his arm, I was able to prevent myself from falling.

"No, I do not. If I had known, I would have told you; I do not want to keep anything from you." His heart was racing, but it was not a result of his lying.

By taking a deep breath and fiddling with my choker necklace, I was able to relax a little. I noticed that the other royals were lying on the ground. "What has happened?"

When Hardin assisted Michael in getting off the ground, he said, "You. I did not even know you could do something like that." He didn't look at me.

Ezra stopped me as I was about to enter the room to assist Jon and Headmaster Grey. "We should rest." he said.

As I shook my head, I replied, "I would rather see my mother and see if my brother is still working at my old school. Or was that bracelet dream true that he left after I arrived here?"

"The bracelet dream?" Headmaster Grey inquired.

"Yes, I know things that I should not know." I nodded.

"I am not sure what you mean. What things do you know?"

"During my bracelet dream, I stopped Ezra from finishing Kolby. Then Hardin and his guards took Kolby and Mortimer, even though Natalia escaped before Hardin arrived. My mother explained that she was aware of who I was. My brother left town right after I left to return home. And Mr G was dressed as Mortimer? Although that is incorrect."

Headmaster Grey agreed, "That is quite unusual."

I took a step back, feeling lightheaded all of a sudden. "I think whatever I did to you guys used a lot of power, and I did not realise." I glanced at Ezra, "I think you are right. I should rest now."

Ezra nodded, "Okay, let's go."

"No, I want you here. Make sure they will be okay." I placed my hand on his chest.

A concerned expression appeared on his face.

"I'll be fine, but I'm not sure about them," I said, gesturing towards the other royals and the headmaster. They were still catching their breath. "They do not appear to be doing well."

"Can I meet you in your room so we can go to dinner together?"

"Yes," I replied. Let's have dinner in my room."

"Do you still worry about your cousin? She said she was fine with us being together." Ezra whispered.

I shook my head and said, "She is lying to us and herself."

"Oh…" Ezra said as he looked down.

"Let's give her some space, okay?" As I placed my hand on his upper arm, I asked. In response to his nod, I turned to walk away.

The headmaster had relocated me to the room I had occupied

in my childhood, located in a completely different area of the campus.

The only thing I remember is that what was here was the home of my family. Our family has owned it since the blessing was bestowed upon us. Then someone, my mother's adoptive parents, turned it into a school for noble vampires and humans. There were a few trusted shifters and fae, but most students were vampires and humans.

Humans were, of course, unaware of the existence of the supernatural world. However, they were so close to the supernatural world. Without technology, it is easier to hide things such as being supernatural.

Slowly, I ascended the steps of the main building. The building my family called home was the main building of the school. As a child, I spent most of my time in the nursery. Or what was once the nursery? That is the room I am currently in.

A light blue and light tan colour scheme dominate the room. I had a canopy bed with a frame resembling a tree's branches in my room. I had white bed sheets to match my white egg chair in the corner beside my nightstand. The chair stood next to a windowsill bench with two bookcases in my reading corner. A loveseat and a desk were on the opposite side of my room. On that loveseat, my father used to read me bedtime stories before leaving for business meetings. As a child, blue was my favourite colour, and it is the colour of my family as well. I requested blue book covers for my books. As the youngest, I received everything I asked for.

I miss my family very much. There is nothing I can do about it. They requested it to remain as statues. I would like to locate Cassius. I would feel better if I did. If my dream were accurate, he would no longer live in that town. I do not know where he will be.

In the same way, I do not know where Katie is. Occasionally, she will provide updates to Renee or the Headmaster. There has been no communication between us. She is going through a lot at the moment. Kit was her mate, but she lost him. Katie got Kit back after our sister, Natalia, possessed Renee's body. Natalia changed her name to Norma after possessing Renee and cast a love spell on Kit. After the spell was broken, he suffered a great deal of pain, and he committed suicide. While Kit was dealing with his pain, I was caught up in my mess. Everyone dealt with my issue.

I felt guilty for not being there to comfort either of them. I was trapped, and my life was drastically altered. Ezra tries to comfort me by saying that no one has noticed Kit's suicide. This makes me feel even worse. He did not have anyone to turn to. He was all alone. Everyone had to deal with Mortimer and me. He suffered the pain he did as a result of our actions.

As I lay on the bed, I closed my eyes. Sighing, I placed my arm over my eyes. There is nothing I can do for my loved ones. Although I could apologise to Kit's parents, I doubt they would recognise me. There have been many changes to my appearance. There are times when I hardly remember myself in the mirror. Sometimes I wish to be the human me, but in reality, I am the vampire me. My previous hair colour was caramel, and my eyes were hazel. Now I have red-brown hair and amber eyes like my dad's. Both my brother and mother have deep hazel eyes and dark brown hair.

I began to get up and leave the room. It had been a long time since I had seen my parents, and I wanted to go see them.

4. The Hidden Past

There is a difference in decoration between the hallways and the other buildings on campus. Whites, tans, golds, and reds dominate it. When Mum was headmistress, she decorated the buildings in this manner. I was a little sickened, even by the minimal decorations she provided throughout the building. After her adoptive mother retired, she became headmistress. As a result of Kolby killing her husband many years ago, her adoptive mother could no longer cope with life.

I walked down to the old animal housing. I walked toward the old animal housing, which housed the supernatural's pets and familiars. There is a new building in which the animals are cared for. There is a large room for every animal with glass walls on all sides.

I carefully stepped on each porch step; they were old, and I did not want them to break under my weight. I entered the building and went through the house to the basement door. The wallpaper wall appeared to be a regular light blue background with cypress flowers—a single framed photograph of Matthew and Grace Thorn, the creators of Knight Academy. Cypress Institute was originally Knight Academy.

Once you have said the Releasing Spell, it becomes a door

leading to the basement. There are only a few people who are aware of the secret basement. I placed my hand on the framed picture. "I give you permission to release the secrets you hide inside. I release you and decree you to show your secrets." The wall melted away, revealing a dark wooden door with an old-fashioned circle handle. As I pushed on the door, it opened.

I felt my stomach drop to the ground.

Once again, it was my fault.

Kolby was awakened from his stone sleep by me. I was responsible.

While biting my lip, I blinked back a few tears. Purebloods do not express their feelings in public. Since I have been a human for so many years, I have become rusty at controlling my emotions. As a result of lashing out at my feelings earlier, I made a mistake. I am losing control of my abilities. No pureblood would do that, whether they were Fae, Shifters, or Vampires.

The steps creaked as I took them one at a time. As old as the foundation of the building, the stairs have been there for centuries. Everything in this room looked the same as the last time I visited. Twenty years have passed since that night. The dust had now covered everything. The statues of my parents were visible to me. They were still asleep in their stone state.

"I did not expect you to come here, Princess."

In the corner, Estrid was seated in a chair, and I was startled when I saw her there.

"What are you doing down here?" I inquired.

"I told the headmaster that I would stay in the old animal housing building," Estrid replied with a shrug. "This used to be where I stayed whenever I visited." As she paused, she looked up at my mum. "My heart longs for her return, and I wish to bring her back to us. Nevertheless, if I were to wake her up too early, she would be extremely pissed off." Looking back at me, she chuckled, "They both have a nasty temper and are very headstrong."

Then I looked at my parents, "I'm sure they would both be furious. And I've heard stories about my dad. It was never something I knew about Mum."

Estrid chuckled, "Yes, your father was a bit of a hothead even though he was 2000 years old."

Looking at her, I asked, "I assume we can only wake them up after Kolby has left?" She nodded. As I continued, I took a deep breath. "But what if we cannot get rid of him, especially with Mortimer, who keeps getting in the way?"

Estrid paused to take a deep breath before walking towards me. Putting her hand on my shoulder, she said, "Listen, kiddo, we will stop him so we can find your brother and then wake up your parents." With her soft voice and appearance, she almost reminded me of my mum.

There was a creak above us. "Has someone followed me?" I asked quietly.

"There are not many people who come here," Estrid replied. "But let's be careful as we leave."

As Estrid turned off the light, I nodded as we headed back up. As I opened the door slowly, I took a moment to look around. There was no one around that I could see or sense. We quickly exited the basement and closed the door. The false wall has regenerated. Estrid inspected the front of the house while I examined the back. Mr Gair, how are you? I was unaware that you were still teaching here." Estrid inquired.

With my vampiric speed, I rushed towards them and asked,

"Mr G, what are you doing here?"

"I saw you walk into the building and wondered why you were here?" he said, shrugging.

I gestured towards Estrid and said, "I was visiting Estrid. Since I had not seen her in a while, I wanted to tell her I was doing well."

When he looked at the fake wall, he asked, "Oh, are those the original owners?" He approached the wall. Estrid shook her head when I looked at her.

Estrid replied, "Yes, they are, indeed. They were great parents to Elizabeth."

"I miss them both," Mr G said as he gazed back at me. I wish you had had the opportunity to visit the school when your mum was the headmistress. She would know how to resolve this Mortimer problem without involving students." He turned his attention back to the picture, "What were you two doing here?" Mr G asked Estrid, "Do you live out here, Estrid?"

"I have always stayed here, remember?" She nodded. "You know, my ability is related to animals."

Nodding, he asked, "Well then, why don't you stay in the newer one?"

"Because it is not meant for people anymore," she explained, shrugging. Unlike the other building, this one had one or two queen beds in the bedrooms for humans to live with the animals full time. The other one had a single room with bunk beds. I knew I would not be comfortable there, nor if I could stay there."

"Yeah, that makes sense. Well, I'll let you two catch up. He patted my shoulder and said, "I just wanted to ensure the princess wasn't in trouble."

Suddenly, there was a flash of students screaming, and then

I saw the smile on Kolby's face.

A gasp escaped my lips as I jumped away. I could not look at him directly as I said, "I am uncomfortable with people touching me since the whole torture thing."

Mr G sadly said, "I'll still be on your side even though you're not a Hunter."

I glanced at Estrid. "I am familiar with that look; your mum also experienced flashes. What did you see, Princess?" Estrid asked.

"There is a problem. I think you should find Cassius. There is something off about Mr Gair. Even my bracelet dream tried to warn me about him." I sighed. "While we are distracted by Mortimer in the past and Kolby in the present, something else must be going on."

"What do you mean by that?" Estrid asked in a concerned tone.

Looking back at the fake wall and then to Estrid, I said, "I believe Mr Gair is working with Kolby. He blocked my ability, so I could only see snippets of what he was doing. I am sure he did not even want me to see anything. Is it possible for you to find my brother and bring him home with your ability? He will likely have to use his charm ability to fend off Mr Gair and Kolby."

"Please stay safe, Princess." Estrid nodded and left the room.

There was a sense of emptiness in the building. As I approached the fake wall, I walked back down to see my parents. Previously, the basement did not feel this heavy.

"I miss you very much. It would be nice if I could bring you back now. I am constantly messing things up," I said to myself, holding back my tears and taking deep breaths to keep my emotions in check. "Maybe if you were here, I would not keep making mistakes this bad. However, you were there that night, and I still made such a mess that we had to hide. I caused the breakup of our family. I also broke apart my other family. Natalia would not have attempted to bond with me and Mortimer without me in the family. Kat wouldn't have lost Kit."

It was the same feeling I had before. It felt as if my heart had been stabbed and dropped. Then I feel a weight on my body that puts all this pressure on me. There was a feeling of shaking throughout the entire building. I was unable to fight the tears any longer. My legs were unable to support me.

"It's all my fault." I sobbed.

5. Atrabilious

It was challenging to put myself back together, but I eventually managed to do so. At least enough to allow me to return to my room. Laying on my bed, I began to relax. My phone was constantly ringing; all the texts were coming through. It is a good thing I did not take it with me. Otherwise, Mr Gair would have heard me in the basement.

4:52 PM

EZRA: I heard about the main building. Are you alright?

4:54 PM

EZRA: Please let me know if you are safe

4:56 PM

HARDIN: Are you in your room? The main building had a terrible earthquake. Half the building collapsed.

5:00 PM

EZRA: Hardin hadn't heard anything from you either. Heading that way.

As I looked at the time, it was 5:32 PM. They were both texted. The wonderers must have already repaired the building. There was nothing out of place that I noticed.

ME: Sorry, I went for a walk and left my phone in my room. I just came back and hadn't noticed anything. Or the building collapsed.

After waiting for a text reply, I heard a knock on the door.

A male voice asked, "Is everyone alright?"

My first response was to open the door and say, "Yes, all is fine."

It was a wonderer at my door. To indicate the severity of their crimes, they wore different coloured cloaks. The colour of this one was black. In general, black is for something small, which means they still have the right to speak. "Are you aware of what happened?" he inquired.

As I shook my head, I replied, "No. I just entered my room. Would you let me know if you have any updates?"

As he nodded, "Yes." he started to walk towards the next room and knocked on the door. I was unaware that people lived here in rooms. These were the rooms of my family and anyone close to us. There was a teacher who popped her head out. She was asked the same question that the wonderer asked me.

I returned to my room. As I turned my back toward the door, I pressed my hands against it.

BEEP BEEP

I received another text message. I expect Ezra or Hardin to reply to me. My phone was lying on my bed, so I went to pick it up.

KAT: How are you?

It felt as if my throat was tightening. I felt as if I was about to lose control once again. Taking deep breaths, I exhaled. I pondered what I would say. 'I'm doing well, miss you. Is your search going well?' or 'I apologise for not being there for you. I wish I could help you.' I have decided to go with the first option. Keep it short and to the point. If I sent the second one, I would lose the little control I possess.

KAT: I'm doing. The search is going pretty well. I'm sorry I haven't been communicating with you. I wanted to wait till I found a good lead. And I think I found it.

ME: Oh, really? That's good!

KAT: Yes! I finally found someone to teach me how to use my Light Matter Magick. Which I read somewhere this person could bring someone back from the dead.

ME: I hope it does. Where is this lead? Maybe I could help?

KAT: I can't tell you yet; I don't know if they will show up. But I'll let you know when I go meet them.

ME: Please do. I don't want anything to happen to you.

KAT: From what I heard, the person I'm meeting up with doesn't usually get out. But when they do, they are always so kind.

ME: When was the last time the person was out?

KAT: Their cousin just visited them yesterday. Everything will be ok; I just wanted to tell you the news first. I have to go now; I'll let you know when I meet with the person.

ME: Ok, I'll talk to you then.

I waited for a few minutes before giving up on a response. I went to my conversation with Ezra.

ME: Do you want to meet in the garden?

EZRA: Sure. What time?

ME: I need a shower. So, like 50 minutes?

EZRA: Yes. That works

6. The Gardens

I strolled through the garden. It has been some time since we last visited. It was during this time that I became a pureblood once again. Blood appeared to cover everything, as I recall.

I looked at him as he squeezed my hand. It appeared that he was concerned. Although it seems like it has been a long time since I became a pureblood vampire, it was only five days ago. On most of those days, I was in recovery and trying to hold down a bag of blood.

During the transformation, purebloods may have difficulty holding back 'old' blood. Until fresh blood is obtained, some purebloods may go insane.

Ezra led us to the fountain where we sat. An angel stands on top of the three-tiered fountain. He gazed into the water as he sat down. "Ezra. I apologise for not answering you." I paused, "I needed to go for a walk."

Ezra tilted his head and asked, "Is everything okay?" Gently patting him next to him, inviting me to sit beside him.

My head nodded as I replied, "Yeah, of course. I have difficulty keeping my emotions in check. You would not think that being a human for a brief period could ruin the control I had built." I paused, looking down. "It's just a lot at the moment.

While adjusting to being back, I'm asked to travel back to the 1990s to battle Mortimer. This is something I never endured as a pureblood."

He squeezed my hand and said, "I will be there. You don't have to fight alone." His gaze remained fixed on mine. "Do you still have those dreams?" He asked.

As I have not yet shared the full details of my dream with him, I did not respond. My gut feeling was that something terrible would happen to him in the middle of the lake. "It remains the same. I cannot understand what the man is saying and what the Valentines have to do with anything. They have turned into humans decades ago as a punishment."

"What if, like you, the spell wore off over time? Are they now plotting revenge against the council for the harm they suffered? As I have heard, they are self-centred and treat anyone below pureblood status poorly." Ezra noted.

I shrugged, "Maybe, but from what I have read and heard about them, they are impatient and do not think things through."

He bumped my shoulder with him, "I was joking. I don't think anything would happen with them. I think they would have done something, or someone would have known something."

The two of us sat in silence. As I gazed up at the sky, I was still becoming accustomed to how bright everything was with my vampire eyes. Getting up in the morning has been challenging. Everyone has been understanding, which is a blessing.

As I rested my head on Ezra's shoulder, I said, "I could get used to the fact that I would not have classes during the day."

In response, Ezra chuckled, "Yes, but remember that Headmaster Grey gave you only two months off."

Sighing, I said, "I wish we could remain in our little garden forever." I glanced at him. The two of us could remain here; we do not need to leave."

His dark chocolate eyes turned red and then turned back to normal, "We can't, or our timeline will be disrupted."

My head was lifted from his shoulder as I shrugged. There is no certainty whether it was us now or in the future. Therefore, it would be best if we did not go now. We should just stay."

"With both of us being purebloods, I am confident we will be able to retrieve him quickly." Ezra mused, watching me closely.

My eyes met with his, "Ezra, I do not think we will make it back together." I looked away, "I haven't been completely honest about the dream I keep having."

After a pause, he asked, "Is that something bad?"

"I am not certain."

"Well, tell me about your dream from beginning to end."

I turned my gaze back towards him and said, "First, I heard a man say, Selene. The only thing I can see of him is behind him; he has the same colour hair as the Knight family. It must be my father since a voice advised that if you accept this gift, you will be damned. In a flash of purple light, I block the light, and the man disappears. There is a woman in his place. Her appearance is similar to that of Selene, the creator of vampires. She says you must free us, princess. As she points behind me, I see you lying in a lake. It seems that something is off. I am unable to move. The same man calls my name when I cannot see anything anymore. His words are broken."

There was a pause.

Ezra said, leaning toward me, "I have faith that you will save me, no matter what." He gently placed his hand on my chin so I could look at him. On my forehead, he places a kiss. "You have the potential to be one of the strongest purebloods. You are a descendant of the original pureblood." He lets me go and gently brushes my cheek with his thumb. He smiles at me, "I trust you completely."

I began to feel dizzy. "I forgot to eat," I said, placing my hand on my forehead.

Ezra nodded, "Okay, let's go." He guided me to the cafeteria.

I could obtain some blood since there was no one in the cafeteria. After that, Ezra walked me to my room and asked, "Are you nervous?"

"What about?" I asked, sipping blood from my baby Yoda mug.

"About the council meeting tomorrow." Ezra paused as we approached the main building.

"That is tomorrow?" I sighed and tilted my head back. There were still a few days left, I thought. I thought we had more time to prepare for the meeting."

As Ezra leaned against the pillar, he shook his head. "That means Renee will be done with her time travel spell by the end of the week."

As I snapped my head towards him, I asked, "What?"

He replied, looking concerned, "Yes, Renee said during our meeting today that she is very close to solving the problem. You weren't paying attention to her."

In response, I shook my head, "I've told you—it has been a long time since my transformation. Even before then."

As Ezra nodded, "I can't imagine. Once we get Mortimer back to the present, Renee and your sister will handle him. Then, you can relax and begin rebuilding your life again, as rapidly as you wish."

31

As I messed with my necklace, I glanced back at him. "Do you think this will be an easy mission?"

"Estrid explained how the events should proceed. As long as we follow her instructions, we should be fine." He smiled and kissed me on the forehead, "Well, it is about time to turn in. We have a meeting; I will meet you in the morning to walk together."

My head nodded in agreement, "Yes, please. I do not want to travel alone."

"I can't go in like last time since you aren't human." Ezra replied, "But I will get as close as possible just in case something happens."

"Thank you," I replied with a nod.

7. The Struggles of a Pureblood

Getting up in the morning was so difficult now that I was a vampire. As I pulled myself from the bed, I felt as though I was ripping myself apart. As supernatural beings, we are generally light on our feet, but I felt so heavy. The Fae walk the softest, especially if they have wings. When in the presence of humans, they will barely touch the ground, but enough to give the impression that they are walking. Because vampires and shifters are nocturnal, they find it difficult to get out of bed in the morning. Although I do not recall it being this difficult as a child.

I chose a soft makeup look while applying makeup. There was a knock at my door. Even before I opened it, I knew who it was. As I opened the door to let him in, I said, "Hello, Ezra. I'm almost done getting ready, if you don't mind waiting in my room."

Ezra smiled and replied, "Okay, that's fine. I believe we still have some time. I was hoping we could stop for breakfast?"

I smiled, "Yeah, though I don't think I can hold down normal food yet."

"That's okay," Ezra replied. "It would be a quick meal, but at least we would spend time together before the meeting."

After nodding, I said, "Of course." and finished getting ready.

As soon as I had finished, we headed to the cafeteria. This was the first time we had been seen together in public. We have been trying to keep it low-key for Freyja's sake and, honestly, for my own. Any type of change can be overwhelming. I took a deep breath as Ezra opened the cafeteria's doors. Fortunately, we arrived early, so few people were in the cafeteria. There was no sign of Freyja. Let's get our quick breakfast and then head out."

Ezra nodded, and we proceeded to line up. As we stood close together, all I could hear was whispers from other students. The whispers were about us and me. It has been a while since I have been in public. It was difficult for me not to listen to them. They were wondering who I was, why I was with the vampire prince, and from what family I came. There were a few people who knew who I was. A gentle brush of Ezra's hand passed over mine, causing me to return my attention to him. "Don't worry about them. It does not matter what they say right now." Ezra said.

In a state of confusion, I asked, "Do they not matter?"

Ezra shook his head and replied, "Nope. Getting food and attending the meeting are the only things that matter now."

I was unsure of what to say. After I nodded, we waited in line for our food. After Ezra got a breakfast burrito, the cook hooked me up with fresh blood since the blood I had been receiving made me weak. Following Ezra outside the cafeteria, I poured it into my little thermos and sat in the gardens away from the crowd. It is common for supernatural beings to eat human food from time to time to practise for the time when they will be mixing with humans.

"Cleo!" Renee shouted. Having portaled to us, she had reached us. She looked frantic and had a mess of white hair.

"The council is here."

I asked, walking towards her. "What happened?"

She bent over and was panting. "I just couldn't figure out where you were." She stood up and said, "They demand to see you. They said you avoided them for too long."

I shrugged my shoulders, "Just trying to get my bearings." I sighed, "I'm guessing they are in the conference room?"

Ezra glanced at Renee as she nodded. "They also wanted to meet with you. "I can portal you there." We both nodded, and she began creating the portal.

8. The Dreaded Meeting

All three of us passed through the portal gracefully. "Are you ready?" I asked Ezra. "I am sure they will not be pleased."

As he nodded, he asked, "When are they ever happy?"

Then I turned to Renee and asked, "Are you coming?"

"No, they wanted to meet with you two," she responded.

As I looked back at Ezra, he nodded in agreement. As he extended his arm to me, I took it. Then I turned back to Renee and said, "See you on the other side."

"Good luck in there," Renee said with a smile. "I know how they are."

In response, I smiled back. As I turned to Ezra, he looked at me. "I will sit as close to the front as possible. I should still be visible. I'll be there if you need help getting out. There shouldn't be any problems. However, my aunt can be petty." Ezra said.

I sighed, saying, "That sucks because I can relate to that. She did believe and house my uncle although he murdered not only my family but other families as well."

As Ezra looked at me, he said, "I would appreciate it if you did not initiate any discussion with the council, particularly my aunt and uncle. It may be tempting."

I nodded, "I understand. As I am no longer human, I am not allowed to be petty?" I turned to leave. While I was unprepared to face the council again, at least the Fae queen would support me. Our families share a common history. She and my vampire grandma were once best friends. In me and my brother's eyes, the Fae Queen had always been a faery grandmother.

Would the Fae Queen say or do anything if she saw through the human spell I was under? Probably not; the Fae are excellent at keeping secrets. Throughout history, vampires, shifters, and hunters have messed up. Though some Fae would tell humans, they generally keep their information to themselves. In most cases, it would be the half-Fae who would divulge any secrets.

"Okay, I think I am ready." I replied.

"Are you sure?" inquired Ezra. "You do not need to be in there yet; we have about ten minutes to go."

"Yeah, I'm ready," I replied. I want to finish this so we can start preparing for the past. After I have completed that, we will be able to relax. "We do not have to do anything if we do not wish to."

As Ezra smiled, he asked, "Where did this come from?"

I shrugged and replied, "I'm not sure, but I'm willing to ride this out."

As he opened the double doors, Ezra nodded. "Okay, then let's go." he said.

It was a large room with a circle of chairs in the centre. We headed toward the centre of the circle, where there was a place where we could walk down. As we walked down the steps, I could feel the pressure of all the council's eyes upon us. As I looked around, I was surrounded by glass, and on the other side of the glass, I could see the four small stadium seats around the room. My friends, academic staff, and students were all visible to me.

As I approached the podium, I waited for any of them to speak to me. My last visit here was so nerve-wracking. I recall my palms being sweaty. However, this time I was on the same level as them. As a result of who my father was, it might even be higher. He was one of the originals, one of the strongest.

My mind flashed back to his stone sleep. As I closed my eyes tightly, I tried to erase the image from my mind. There is no way that I can remember him that way right now, or I will lose control over my emotions. After taking a few breaths, I opened my eyes once again.

Even if I cannot tell the full truth, I must tell my truth.

9. The Tales of Maria Knightley

The podium was moved so that I faced the Fae Queen. She smiled and said, "It's nice to see you again, dear. I am glad that you were able to find your way home." In addition to having pale blonde hair with pink stripes, she had a shortcut similar to a bob. The colour of her eyes was the same shade of pale pink.

In response, I smiled and said, "I am glad to be back as well. It has been 20 years since I last saw you."

A 180-degree turn was made by the podium so that I would face the Alpha of the shifters. I can see where Micheal gets his look from. Greetings, princess. You may not remember me, but I am Janet Balus."

I shook my head and replied, "No, I do not believe I know you. It is a pleasure to meet you."

As Janet pointed to the man beside her, she said, "This is Ron Balus, my mate." Ron waved but did not speak.

"I am not sure whether this is appropriate. As a human, I had a best friend named Ronnie." I could see Janet tensing up. That provided me with all the information I needed. I knew the others would be confused about why I would ask, "It's neat that she has the same last name."

Then, a slight turn to the left was made on the podium to

face Jon's father. Their features are identical, with short hair and brilliant hazel eyes. As Jon faked a smile, he said, "Hello, Princess. My name is Jon; I believe you have already met my son." He gestured to the man beside him and said, "This is my right hand, Rick."

I smiled back and said, "Nice to meet you both. I am glad that hunters now have representation on the council; however, I regret missing out on the history of hunters."

Short and sweet.

"Maria Knightley, we are here today to determine what really transpired the night your family was murdered." Jon Jackson, the Hunter Leader, began.

"It is Cleo; that has always been my name," I said and saw the confusion on most of their faces. "It is common for the Knight family to hide their first daughter's name to keep her safe from anyone putting a curse on her. Despite my best efforts, I am still attempting to recall my life as a pureblood."

"So, can you tell us anything about that night your family was murdered?" Jon asked, annoyed. "Did you have a role to play?"

"Well, I had been visiting a statue in our basement for weeks. This was in the home we lived in before it was converted into the teachers' dormitory for the school. It was still the home of the Knight family, with some of the staff staying as well. I had been using my ability to communicate with the person inside the statue and become friends. According to him, my parents were trying to assist him, but they could not. An individual with a long bloodline and the blood of an original is what they need. He informed me that my parents did not want to guilt me into helping them with their problems. As a result, I decided to assist him. As it turns out, the statue was, in fact, my uncle in a stone sleep. To keep me safe from the danger he was about to bring to our family, he put me into a small sleep spell for a short period of time. In my memory, I remember waking up earlier than he expected; I recall a monster chasing after me and my brother." My heart was racing as I recalled the burnt-looking monsters chasing us. As I looked down, I took a deep breath. "My uncle admitted everything to me when I was held captive."

"Does your uncle possess the same abilities as you?" Jon inquired.

"All pureblood Knights possess psychic abilities. While there are a few who do not." I replied.

As Jon raised an eyebrow, he asked, "Like your brother?" He asked, "Speaking of which, where is your brother? Maybe he would bring more light to what happened that night than the little princess could."

I narrowed my eyes and replied, "I have no idea. My brother had been moving around a lot to avoid Kolby.

Jon smirked, "I thought all purebloods knew where everyone in your family was."

"I am not sure what you are trying to prove," I said with a shrug. "We would communicate if we knew each other was alive. However, I do not believe he is aware of me."

Jon narrowed his eyes, "I'm just trying to get the full story."

I narrow my eyes, "Yeah, you guys did an excellent job when Kolby and Mortimer tried to get me last time."

I noticed that the vampire queen and king were not present. Perhaps it has something to do with my uncle, Kolby Knight, who had a hand in killing the Knight family though there isn't proof. "As you may have noticed, the vampire queen and king are not present here." The podium moved towards Janet.

41

As I nodded, I asked, "What happened to them?"

In response, the leader raised her eyebrows and asked, "Ezra, did you not know?" I shook my head. "Both his aunt and uncle are being dethroned." The leader paused, "You are going to take their places since you are the last member of the Knight Clan."

10. Janet Balus, Friend or Foe?

My gaze was drawn to Ezra, who was not making eye contact with me. "When were you going to tell me?"

"Nobody told me; I didn't know." Ezra said, as confused as I was.

I looked at the council and said, "I do not wish to rule. That was my mother's plan for my brother and me. It is my intention to keep it that way."

"I would like to know if he is still alive. Since the night Cypress Institute was attacked in 2003, no one had seen or heard from him." Jon explained.

"I have a gut feeling that my brother is still alive." I said.

As the podium turned to face the Summer Fae Queen, Clarissa Hughes said, "Sweetie, you must prepare yourself to lead the Night Court. It is your time to find your mate and rule."

The podium turned to face Janet, "Or forfeit and let the Night Trials begin."

All three Night Creatures were under the authority of the Queen of the Night Court, namely Shifters, Tribloods, and Vampires. Some Tribloods belong to the Fae Courts. But only if their family is Fae, as most Tribloods are from Vampire or

Shifter families. The Queen or King of the Night Courts must be a pureblood.

"But it is not yet time for Night Trials; there are still four more years to go before they are held." I replied.

"The Vampires have ruled the Night Courts for a long time," Janet stated. "The trials are about due."

"This means the Hunters can take part this time since we now have a seat on the Council." Jon spoke up as the podium turned towards me.

The Night Court is open only to purebloods, so yes, you are eligible for it. I shrugged and said, "If you wish to participate in the Night Trails and fight for it, go for it. I prefer to follow in my mum's footsteps and become the assistant to the headmaster. As it has been too long since I have been away, I would like to be able to stay at home."

The podium turned to face Janet. "You and your mother are always on your damn high horses." Janet growled. "Throughout her life, she has always considered herself too good for the court. It is a part of your blood, so why deny a part of yourself? What makes you believe that you are a Knight?"

There was something off about the sudden change.

Together with the other Council members, I looked at Janet in confusion. "I do not claim to be a Knight since I am a Knightley. I would not consider myself above the law."

Janet appeared to be annoyed as she stood up and jumped towards me. A gasp was heard from the council, and I stepped back. "You are just a spoiled princess who doesn't know what she wants. Your position on the throne would have been secured if you had simply remained by my side. I know you are more like your father when it comes to power, so you could have taken over the world. Janet gestured towards my whole being. "Look at you; you possess so much of it." She continued, "Can you control your thirst since you awoke?" Janet stepped closer, "You are much weaker than you used to be."

Suddenly, Ezra appeared next to me and went to grab her, "What are you doing, Council member?"

She pushed him away, "I am not a member of the Council." She turned back towards me; I reached for her, and she grabbed hold of my hand. There are flashes of Janet's memories and my uncle's memories.

"Kolby?" I whispered. "How are you managing the shifter leader?" The council members were asking each other what I had said.

Someone must bring the wonderers to us!" Headmaster Grey shouted.

Janet smiled, "It took you too long, niece." She paused and released my hand. Her eyes turned a burning orange as she recalled, "You used to be able to see memories without touching them. Look at what being a human did to you, little princess." Janet looked at me with sympathy as her eyes returned to their normal hazel. "I could train you. But you would have to do something for me."

I shook my head, "Sorry, I'm not in the business of making deals with old men any more."

"Then, you will have to be weak," Janet said, annoyed. "Release this blockage that is keeping you from being your true self."

"I am healing from being human for so long." I murmured.

As Janet folded her hands, she sighed. The past must be let go to be able to return to the past. There is a possibility that everyone you love will be injured or killed if you go."

As my eyes widened, I asked, "How did you know?"

There was a sense of sympathy in her voice, "Things have already been set into motion since you are going back in time to the past. This is not going to end well for you."

"Why are you concerned? You have attempted to kill my family three times at this point." I replied.

She looked down to the ground, "No matter how much I hate it, I owe my life to you."

Janet and I were surrounded by the wonderers in their various coloured robes. One of them shouted, "Janet, please raise your hands slowly."

11. As Deep As Hell

Her eyes were glowing orange, and she slowly transformed into her animal form. Winds began to blow, and they were very loud. The closer you got to Janet, the faster the winds became.

Although Ezra, Hardin, Michael, Renee, and Miri remained. My friends and the headmaster, teachers, and nurses were trying to get everyone out. However, they refused to move.

I looked at Michael. "What's your mum's animal?" I yelled.

"She's a wolf but huge." Michael yelled back.

I struggled with Micheal the first encountered him in wolf form, but I was also a human at the time. There was an explosion of black smoke. And Janet's wolf form stood in the centre of the smoke. Her fur was dark brown and her eyes were glowing orange. "Princess, it has been a long time since I have seen you." But the voice wasn't Janet's.

"Kolby?" I asked, backing away from the wolf walking towards me.

"Of course, who else would it be?" Kolby asked, "Unfortunately, I can't greet you in person. I just barely got in range to get a hold of this shifter's mind." As the wolf walked towards me, its gaze was fixed on me.

"I did not realise it was possible to take control of someone's body without being in it." I was as far back as possible while remaining in the centre.

"You have much more power than your parents have taught you." the wolf smiled. "Sebastian being your father, you will be able to do more than I ever could have imagined."

I shook my head, "I don't have that much power."

The wolf shook its head and replied, "Of course you do. You need to let go and believe in yourself. You could easily take me right now. As well as the entire council."

"Maybe, but even if I were able to. I do not wish to fight any more," I was cut off by Headmaster Grey.

"It is time for you to leave, Kolby." The headmaster said, "No one wants you here, and I'm sure Janet would not approve of you taking over her body."

The wolf shrugged, "It doesn't matter what she or anyone wants besides me and Cleo."

As the headmaster helped me out of the pit, he asked, "What do you want from Cleo?"

The wolf paused momentarily, "She needs to be with her family. As soon as she awakens, her power will be unstable. I have felt it since a couple of days ago and last night." As the wolf turned towards me, it said, "I am certain anyone with Knight blood has felt it."

"Why would I want to be with the person who murdered my family?" I asked, standing back up.

The wolf narrowed its eyes, "Because I'm the only family you have left."

As I shook my head, I said, "Not true. In fact, I have a new family now."

The wolf appeared to be bored. "Yes, people/ who cannot handle a fraction of the power you harness. What happens if you lose control?"

"Then they can put me back in the hourglass spell again."

"Is that right? Is that where you had been in that short period?" The wolf asked, "I was wondering how you went off-grid." The wolf paused, "That would not work for very long, not with your power. Now, you must choose the easy path or the difficult path. Regardless, you will be with me in the end."

"Why do you care?" I asked.

"It is because you will follow in your father's footsteps. Destruction. You may think it is terrible now, but wait until the power is too much for you to handle. It happened to your father once."

I shook my head, "No, my dad was the best man ever."

The wolf laughed, "Yeah, says the child. Your father's secrets were never revealed to you as a child. As well as your mother. Double edge swords, they were."

"No, you're lying." I could feel that weight once again. I felt as if my heart was being repeatedly stabbed. I was on the verge of losing control.

"You're losing control right now."

I shook my head in disbelief; everything was fine. All I need to do is work on my breathing.

"Cleo?" I could hear Ezra's voice. As I looked up at him, he appeared to be very concerned. "It's ok, Cleo. The teachers can handle your uncle, so let's go to the garden or something."

"Please give me a moment." I closed my eyes again, trying to concentrate on my breathing.

"Is this your soulmate?" The wolf asked.

As I opened my eyes, I saw the wolf grinning at Ezra and Ezra slowly backing away. Because this was not actually Kolby,

I knew he did not want to fight. He could not do use his ability against Janet or Kolby. He would be in trouble for endangering a pureblood. It would be a decent amount of time as a wonderer, but not as long as it would be if you were to kill a pureblood. There are fewer of us than before.

The headmaster rushed to the area and intervened between Ezra and the wolf. "No, you must stop."

"Yeah?" the wolf laughed. "What will you do?" The wolf swats the headmaster away. The headmaster slammed into the wall. In tears, Nurse Grey, his wife and soulmate, rushed to the headmaster.

While Janet was scratching me, Ezra jumped in front of me. "No, Ezra!" I yelled as he fell on top of me. While on the floor, I attempted to get up and check his back, but nothing was found. As we both stood up, I felt a sense of relief. Without harming Janet, the Wonderers attempted to fight off Janet.

"Ezra, what were you thinking? A scratch from a shifter could do us great harm." I squeezed his hand as we attempted to escape the Meeting Hall.

Janet leapt into the air in front of us. Ezra loaded a bright green ball of kinetic energy into one hand and pushed me behind him with the other. "Cleo, come with me. It is possible for you to change the future; you could rule the courts." Janet hissed.

"She isn't going with you! Haven't you caused her enough pain?" Ezra said. As Janet approached, the surviving Wonderers stood in her way. As a result of their powers, the wonderers battled Janet. "Ezra, Cleo!" The headmaster yelled. We looked back; someone had made a portal.

11. AS DEEP AS HELL

12. As High as Heaven

Headmaster Grey was the only Council Member who had yet to go through. At first, Ezra hesitated, but he eventually followed me to the portal. I could hear the screams of the wonderers; I looked back to see Janet flying toward us in the air. Knowing that I would have to do something, I held out my hands and forced energy toward Janet to knock her from the sky.

Instead, I created a shield of light grey. The shield appeared to be protected by electricity around me and Ezra. With every hit or attack, she made on the shield, I felt the force pushing my arms downward. When someone arrived, I tried to hold it until they could get her away. Breathing became increasingly difficult.

I have never been trained for combat. Dad always promised me, but he could never fulfil his promise. As my knees could not bear the weight of the attacks, Ezra rushed to assist me in getting back up. "Let me strike her with my kinetic energy."

In response, I shook my head, "She is still a pureblood. You will hurt her if you attack her with your abilities." I turned to him, "I cannot lose you as well."

"I have to do something. There is no way you can hold her off for too long. It has been a long time since you have been a pureblood." Ezra said, holding me up.

"I guess there is a difference between Elizabeth and you, little princess. She could fight me moments after waking up from the human curse." Janet hissed. "When did you return? Two to three weeks?"

As I clenched my jaw, I shouted, "Keep my mother's name out of your mouth!" I exhaled deeply and focused on what was inside. I am aware of my breathing, my thoughts, and my heartbeat. An ashy blue string could be seen; this must be my soul's string.

As I placed one of my hands towards my side, I imagined that same blue colour becoming a ball in the palm of my hand.

I tossed the ball towards Janet; the ball was actually a light grey colour, the same colour as the shield. "So, you *can* control your Dark Matter Magick." Janet murmured in response. The ball engulfed Janet; I could hear her screams. By calling the energy from the ball and shield back to me, I received it. Janet's eyes caught my attention as I looked down at my blood-stained hand. Janet was slashed by my ball of Dark Matter Magick.

As I turned toward Ezra, he was in a state of shock. The headmaster grabbed both of us and dragged us towards the portal.

Janet grabbed Ezra, and the headmaster pushed me into the portal, causing me to land on my back.

Looking around, I discovered I was in the hospital wing. Several people were rushing around to ensure that everyone received treatment. In the distance, I noticed Ron Balus staring into the abyss. Looking back, I noticed that the portal had disappeared. In a panic, I said, "I must return to Ezra."

Nurse Grey placed her hand on my shoulder, "They will both return to us."

I shook my head, "No, Janet is still being controlled by Kolby."

Ron raised his head and asked, "Is that why she is acting so strange? Because of fucking vampire family drama?" Ron stood up. "There's always something going on with the Knight Family. Ever since the supernatural was created! The Knights are responsible for the existence of supernatural beings."

"I wouldn't have to feel so drained because my soulmate is fighting for her life while your goddamn uncle controls her mind."

"What are you talking about?" I asked.

"I am referring to your progenitor and his relationship with Selene. There is always a Knight at the centre of everything. It should have been the Knights who mysteriously became humans, not Valentines or Gainnes. They were great families and did not look down upon anyone." Ron continued, but Nurse Grey stepped before him to prevent him from getting too close to her.

My dream… Was it real, or was it just a dream?

"Listen to me, Ron. She lost her family when she was a child and has nothing to do with what her family had done in the past." Nurse Grey stated as she began to lead him to his bed. "Please sit down. I'm sure they will all come back." Nurse Grey looked at me. "Please remain here."

I shook my head, "I can't." I slowed my breathing and held out my hand as colours started to swirl around me.

13. The Pull to do Good

The smell of blood overwhelmed me as I stepped through the portal. It was difficult to focus on anything other than the blood. Slowing my breathing and focusing, I noticed that Ezra had backed into the wall. Looking at Ezra, the wolf smiled and attempted to bite him. Despite this, Ezra managed to keep his jaws open. In response to Hardin's spell casting, Ezra yelled, "No! You can't hurt her. She isn't doing this. Plus, you wouldn't forgive yourself for hurting her."

Hardin turned to look at Michael, who stood in a state of fear. I couldn't see Miri anywhere; Hardin probably asked her to leave. Hardin began to pull Michael away to a nearby portal.

My heart began to race. It felt as if I was useless. I cannot control my abilities enough to help my soulmate without losing control completely. As I ran down to the podium area, the blood flow became overwhelming. I created a second portal to pull Headmaster Grey through since he was the worst. "Hudson!" Nurse Grey shrieked as I placed Hudson on the ground and walked back into the portal to retrieve Ezra. As I rushed up the stairs, I could barely catch my breath. "Come to me, Cleo, and I will leave Ezra alone." Janet hissed.

"No, you must stop before you cause any further damage.

Janet is already fighting for her life, and you have killed many more people today." I responded. It was time to push my uncle out of Janet's body and mind.

Several portals opened in the room, and some guards from various races began to approach the wolf. Some blows were landed, but not enough to cause the wolf any concern. Kolby does not feel the pain. However, Janet does.

Ezra yelled in pain.

I felt my heart drop. I must take action. Inhaling and exhaling, I focused on the wolf and tried to enter its mind. From a distance, I held my hand out in an attempt to reach Janet's mind. There was an ashy blue string ahead of me that I could see, and I followed it. I was surrounded by a total blackness, and I began to feel that weight again. Similar to what I experienced with Michael, a soft green light appeared. In my attempt to reach for it, something, or someone, slapped my hand away. "You, stupid girl." Kolby hissed. "Do you think that using your power is a wise idea?" We were in the basement, where it all started. But we weren't there. That's the only memory we share together.

I shrugged, leaning against a pillar, "It will get you out of Janet and ensure Ezra doesn't-"

Kolby rolled his eyes, "I had hoped you would come the easy way. However, you are making this a challenging task for me."

"I don't want to go with you; I much rather end you."

Kolby shook his head, "You cannot end a pureblood."

"You said it yourself, my father is an original, and I, as his daughter, will have even greater power than him."

I felt pressure on my body, which was taken from Janet's mind as he smiled, "You have learned your first lesson. Knights get whatever we want. We will always have a pull over everyone else."

It took me a moment to realise I was on the other side of the room.

Janet launched herself towards me at full speed. Using my Dark Matter Magick, I summoned a small shield. As soon as Janet hit the shield, she fell backwards. I approached her with my vampiric speed and placed a hand on the wolf's head.

Janet's memories surrounded me, and I searched until I found her. "Janet?" I asked as she turned around to face me. She immediately lost her smile upon seeing me. On the beach, she was sitting with her mate, Ron. Her confusion was followed by a moment of realisation.

She jumped to her feet and said, "I promise that isn't me! There is no way I could ever hurt as many people as I have."

Holding my hand, I smiled softly, "Let's fix this, shall we?"

Despite Janet's scepticism, she asked, "Can you force him out? I believed you had not yet gained control over your abilities."

I shrugged, "I'm willing to try if you are."

Janet reached out slowly. "What are you doing, Sweets?" Memory Ron asked. As Janet turned back toward him, she said, "I am so sorry, my love." Janet grabbed my hand and began to cry.

14. The Fall of all Good

Then, as if swept away by a hurricane, Janet screamed, "Don't let go of me." I felt our hands slipping, but we returned to the Meeting Hall when we were almost forced apart. Slowly, Janet reverted to her human form.

Looking around, she realised the extent of the damage that she had caused. "Did I do all this?" she inquired.

"I would say yes and no." Standing, I said, "Kolby had control over your body." It was then that I noticed Ezra waking up behind me. I rushed toward him and asked, "Are you all right? Have you been bitten or scratched?" I asked, looking him over.

He shook his head, "No, Lady Janet threw me into the wall." He began to get up but winced as he did so.

'Let's get you to Nurse Grey.' I helped him up, and I could see the pain on his face. "Are you sure you didn't get bit?"

Ezra nodded, "I'm sure."

We stepped through a portal that I opened. Some wonderers followed. There was no doubt that the nurses had their hands full. In a rush, those who were not treating someone rushed toward the few of us who had walked through the portal. "Thank Goddess, both of you are okay." Nurse Grey ran towards us and assisted me in moving Ezra to a makeshift cot. "What happened?"

"I was thrown against a wall." Ezra said, "I should be fine once I get some blood and heal."

Nurse Grey responded, "Let me see if there are any left." She walked back to the back room where the medicines were stored.

Holding his hand as I sat next to him, I asked, "Are you sure?" I said, looking down at his hands. Although they were bruised, the bruises were slowly healing. Although they should already have healed. Some of the venom likely entered his bloodstream.

"Am I certain about what?" Ezra said, his voice was quiet compared to the chaos around us.

The room became silent, and I noticed Janet walking through the portal. An individual with blue eyes and blonde hair who was a council member approached Janet. He clenched his fists and commanded, "Answer this, Council Member Janet." He paused and asked, "Why? What motivated you to attack us on this day?"

As Janet stared down, her voice broke. "I-" She said sheepishly. Tears were slowly rolling down her cheeks. "I was unable to control my body." She covered her face with her hands as her mate approached to hug her.

"What do you mean by that?" the man asked. He must have been the secondhand for the tribloods, Rick.

Janet continued to shake her head as she began to cry more intensely. Janet was watched for a considerable time.

"Sir, she was possessed by my uncle." I said without emotion.

The man looked at me and asked, "How could your uncle have possessed someone? The man is not a witch."

I nodded, "But he has been working with witches since the attack on the school 20 years ago."

59

"Who would want to work with Lord Kolby after he had been blacklisted?" The man asked.

"I could not tell you since I have lived as a human for most of my life." I shrugged, "But shouldn't the Council be aware of what is happening in the supernatural community?"

His eyes were fixed on the ground as he thought for a moment.

A man's voice spoke up, "Let's investigate." Jon, the hunter leader, stepped forward. "It was our responsibility as hunters to figure things out for the council. Being a member of the council does not change that fact."

The blonde man, Rick, nodded, "You're right, Leader."

"Rick, come on. Let's get started; we have a lot of work to do." Jon said. Before stepping through the portal, Jon looked back at me and said, "You take care, Princess. I ask you not to cause any more trouble."

"I seem to be in trouble all the time." I replied.

As he and Rick stepped through the portal, Jon smiled.

Several days had passed since the attack. Most of the injured had healed relatively quickly and returned to normal. Well, not entirely normal, as the meeting hall was utterly destroyed. Ezra was in a coma for two days after a high fever. It is still my fear that he may fall back into one. There was some shifter saliva in his wound from the teeth, but not enough to cause death. It was no longer necessary for him to remain in the hospital wing.

To make a better antidote for Ezra, Janet donated some of her blood to Nurse Grey. The Council Members had left that evening after the attack. Kolby had somehow gained control of Janet's body, so they had to figure out how he had done so.

As Ezra tightened his grip on my hand, he said, "You do not have to remain by my bed. Trust me, I will be fine."

I narrowed my eyes at him and said, "You are still sick. Vampires do not become ill, Ezra."

Ezra smiled lightly, "I am not as sick as I was. Thanks to Nurse Grey for making those anti-venom pills."

"Yes, you have improved. But still not in top shape and-" I was interrupted by a ding, ding.

I looked at it as I pulled my phone from my back pocket.

"Who is it?" Ezra asked, getting in a sitting position in his bed.

I read the text, "It's from Hardin. He said he got everyone together for a royal meeting, and it's happening here in 30 minutes."

"Okay, then, let's get ready." He said, getting out of bed.

Then I grabbed his shirt and said, "Hey, be careful not to overwhelm yourself. Okay?"

He nodded.

15. The Last We Meet

We were in the royal meeting room, which is located in the main building. Hardin and Michael sat across from one another at the coffee table next to the fireplace. Ezra and I sat across from the fireplace on the couch. As Renee stood in front of the fireplace, she paused momentarily. Ezra and I laced our fingers together. A feeling of normal sparks is present. When we made eye contact, I smiled at him.

Keeping his hand on my cheek, he smiled and brushed my reddish-brown hair out of my face. "Thank you for saving me."

"Of course!" I said softly.

"Ezra," Hardin said after clearing his throat. Ezra looked up at Hardin for a moment. "I would like to thank you for saving us."

Ezra nodded but looked at me and said, "Cleo is the real hero. Cleo was able to control her powers extremely well."

Another pause followed.

"Well, Princess, it's your turn to begin." Hardin replied.

Taking a deep breath, I squeezed Ezra's hand and then released it. Standing up, I walked toward the fireplace so everyone could see me. The headmaster wasn't here; he was still severely injured. Nevertheless, the Hunter Prince, Jon

Reyes, the Shifter Prince, Michael Balus, the Fae Prince, Hardin Hughes, and the Heir's Guardian, Renee Page, were present. Although Miri, Hardin's girlfriend, is usually present at these meetings, she was absent.

"So, we planned to travel back in time in a few months. However, after Kolby's attack, we should do it this week, preferably tonight." I stated. "I do not want another attack to disrupt our travel plans. In addition, I believe there are too many threats with Mortimer in the past and Kolby attacking the school right now."

"How much control do you have over your powers? This was the primary reason we waited so long." Jon asked, his eyes narrowing.

"I was able to save both Ezra and the headmaster. I believe I have finally understood my power." I stated.

"There would not have been as many deaths if you controlled your powers. I thought your father was all-powerful. Are you sure you are of Knight blood?" Jon asked.

"I am, but I also haven't had my whole life to fill in his shoes yet. Did you forget that I was human for most of my life?" I asked him.

"If you were actually a Knight, being human shouldn't significantly impact your powers. I have heard stories about Lady Elizabeth when she was changed back. In no time at all, she was able to slip back into her role as a pureblood vampire. In that case, what is wrong with you?" Robert asked.

"Leave her alone." Ezra advised.

Jon raised his hands innocently, "I'm just making sure she can handle herself before we send her to the past."

"I saw her that day; she appears to have a handle on her power." said Ezra.

He tilted his head, "Did she really have control over her powers? Was it a miracle that her power did not worsen the situation?"

I narrowed my eyes at him, his mannerisms reminding me of Mortimer. The memory of Mortimer flashed through my mind, the rage he caused me to feel. There was no doubt that Mortimer knew how to push my buttons, and I honestly let him do so. As a result, I fell into every trap he set for me; I followed his instructions without intending to do so. I wanted revenge on Mortimer for ruining my peaceful life as a human being. My desire to harm both Kolby and Mortimer is intense. They both ruined everything around me.

I turned my attention to Renee and said, "Please, send me back in time. Until I can kill both Mortimer and Kolby, I will not be able to rest."

"You will not be killing either, Cleo." Jon responded, "Mortimer is under our ranks. As for Kolby, you cannot kill him because he is a pureblood vampire."

Through my peripheral vision, I asked, "Has that prevented him from killing my family? Moreover, if he is under *your* rule, why are you not the one to take him into custody? Why would you send a vampire to perform your duties?"

Jon looked away.

Looking back at the group, I said, "I would like to return to the past tonight. Besides, I do not want anything else to delay the event further."

Everyone paused for a moment.

"OK, I will do it." Renee replied.

"Thank you, Renee." With excitement, I grabbed Ezra's hand.

Renee said, as she headed towards the bookcase, "I need you to follow me." She slightly pulled out a book about the

Guardians and the Divine, and the bookcase slid back to reveal a pocket world. There were several portals in this room. It reminded me of the Gathering, but there were portals instead of large stones blocking the centre. Instead of a bonfire, the centre had a small house.

"What is this place, Renee?" Hardin asked.

Renee smiled, "Do you think the Fae Prince is the only person capable of creating pocket worlds?" Renee walked towards the house. The house was a studio with a table, fireplace, bed, kitchen, and a small bathroom. "The spell must be continuously performed. As a result of taking something from each of you, we are the only ones who can reach this world. It will be necessary to have someone check that the spell is still functioning so that you and Ezra can return when it's finished."

"But what about Mortimer?" Robert asked, "If only we could come to this world, how would Mortimer do so?"

Renee stated flatly, "He will not return. Estrid finds his body as it is turning to ash, but he is marked as unknown as no one at that time could identify him."

Jon asked, "How do you know it's Mortimer?"

"When we leave this world, I can show you a picture. There was an article about the mysterious male discovered on the school grounds." Renee stated. As she turned towards me and Ezra, she asked, "Are you ready to return now?"

Ezra looked at me as I looked at him. Nodding, we both agreed. We all headed back to the library room.

16. Curiouser and Curiouser

L ooking at her, I asked, "If there are any questions, how may I contact you?"

Renee pulled out this small gold bracelet, which twisted the metal together. There was a small green gem locket attached to it. As she threw it at me, I was able to catch it. When I noticed the locket could be opened, I opened it to reveal a mirror. "It will not work now, but once I cast the spell, it should begin to work. But use that mirror to contact me." She said. As I looked back at her, she showed me a bracelet she was wearing with the same design as ours. "I will use this one to connect with yours, and we will be able to communicate this way." she said, pointing to the bracelet she was wearing. "If the bracelet falls off your wrist, it will automatically disconnect. I can't risk it falling into the hands of someone in the past. I'm afraid they might try and learn things about the future. Better safe than sorry."

"That makes sense." I put on the bracelet, which caused me to take note of my clothes. It was still my school uniform that I wore last night. "I don't think students wear a uniform like this."

Hardin nodded, "I agree with you. This is why I brought this item for you to wear. In those days, the school was smaller, so you will not be students." Hardin produced a dress bag from nowhere. He unzipped the bag. It was a dark red mesh long-sleeve shirt with black faux leather pants. Hardin handed me the bag.

Hardin handed Ezra another bag. Ezra wore a black button-up with black slacks and a leather jacket.

I went to the next room to put on my clothes. Formerly a men's parlour, it is now used as an office or a private meeting room. A meeting room has been converted from the former lady's parlour.

Someone knocked on the door, "Come in." I said.

It was Renee.

Renee smiled, "I'm glad the colour looks great on you. Some guy suggested it, but we were unsure. He said your mother used to wear something similar."

My head snapped to her, "What guy?"

Renee shrugged, "I am not sure; he said he used to know you when you were a kid. We invited him to join us, but he stated that it was unsafe for you two to be close now."

"Did he have dark hazel eyes and brown hair? He appears to be in his mid-twenties?" I asked.

Renee seemed perplexed, "So, you used to know him?"

Nodding, I felt relieved, "I did. In fact, I sent Estrid to find him; I'm glad he is safe."

"Oh, that's where Estrid went? Who was that?" Renee asked.

I nodded, "But it's better to wait to know till Kolby is taken care of."

Renee nodded, "Oh, I see." Renee messed with her bracelet, "Ok, now that your outfit is on." She opened a small dark blue box and waited for me to put the necklace there. "Put your family's necklace in this box."

I placed my choker in the box. It was strange not to have it around my neck where it is usually located.

I nodded, and we returned back to the pocket world. Ezra commented, having put on his new outfit, "The outfit looks great on you, Cleo."

"I guess my mother wore something similar." I replied.

"Did you know that red is the colour of my family? The fact that your mother wore red makes sense. When your mother was a child, Lady Elizabeth was protected by my mother." Hardin continued.

I looked back at him, "Oh, I didn't know that."

"Lady Elizabeth often referred to my mother as her Faery Godmother."

As I placed my hand on his upper arm, I smiled. I drew a deep breath. It never occurred to me that talking about my mother in such a casual manner would be so painful. I was unsure of what to say to Hardin. "Your mother is the same way for my brother and me."

A pause followed.

Renee and Jon appeared awkward, "Anyways." Renee broke the silence. "Ezra, Cleo, are you ready?"

Nodding, I glanced back at Hardin and Michael. Hardin looked into the fire while Michael looked at Renee and me.

Renee nodded as she began to cast the spell.

The spell was in a Fae language, so I could not understand what she was saying. Ezra and I were surrounded by swirling dark purple smoke. As I squeezed Ezra's hand, I wanted to ensure we would not be separated. I felt like I could not breathe; my lungs were sucked dry. I could tell that Ezra was going through the same experience. My body was squeezed and then torn apart. Although the pain almost led me to give up,

I knew that I should not. I was uncertain whether I was holding Ezra's hand or even standing. Suddenly, a portal appeared; it looked different from the typical portal. With this one, you can actually see where you are going. This was the fountain located in front of the school.

The portal opened, and I stepped through it.

17. 1989

We were almost torn apart from each other. Ezra, however, grabbed hold of my clothing and my arms. I clenched both of his arms tightly. The two of us held on tightly until we crashed into a stone. The water had soaked me completely, I glanced around, and we were standing near the school's main building. Dedicated to my mother's adoptive parents when her name was Brianna. As far as I could tell, the fountain was not damaged. I shielded my eyes from the sun's bright light and gazed at Ezra. It appeared that he was in pain, so I knelt and moved towards him. "Are you ok?" I asked.

In response, he nodded, "Yeah. I just took most of the landing."

"Oh, I'm sorry. My eyes were closed." I replied, placing a hand on his shoulder and gently lifting him.

As he placed his other hand on my cheek, he smiled softly and looked behind me. "I think we should leave before someone comes to investigate what happened."

I looked around me. The two of us were in the gardens at Cypress. Why were we here? Initially, I thought Renee would have dropped us in the middle of the Haunted Forest. The forest that engulfs the island, Staros. Staros is where Cypress

Institute is located. It was only when the Vikings rediscovered the island that it was named Staros. Because the Vikings were unaware of the supernatural beings living on the island, the forest is referred to as the Haunted Forest.

I looked at Ezra worried, "We aren't supposed to be at the school."

"Well, let's hurry and leave campus," Ezra said. "My family used to own a sanctuary in Woemi where supernatural beings could hide."

"Hey!" I heard someone shout. My attention was drawn to the person who saw us.

It was my dad.

I wanted to turn around and hug him so tightly. It was so hard for me to live without him and Mum. It was my fault that they were stuck in a stone sleep. I could feel the ground shake which made Dad stop and look at us, shocked. "Cleo." Ezra said, bringing me back to the present. As I looked toward where we were running, the ground stopped shaking. Before we turned the corner, I noticed a woman I did not know standing with Dad, watching me run.

Once we reached Woemi, people stared at us strangely, but the stares didn't last long. The town of Woemi had a small-town feel, with cobblestone roads and brick buildings. Not much has changed in the present day, except maybe some of the buildings have been upgraded. However, I have not visited Woemi, though I intend to do so in the near future. I looked at the sign of this dark red brick building as Ezra guided us to it. The place was known as Grim Goat. A picture of a goat holding a scythe was on the building's sign.

It turned out to be a bar, and Ezra let go of my hand and approached the bartender. "Yesterday, I disappeared. Today, I shelter. Tomorrow, I will be gone." Ezra whispered.

The bartender appeared confused, but the bartender next to him appeared to understand. "Ah, right away, sir!" The other bartender said, "If you don't mind following me."

As Ezra glanced at me, he tilted his head to indicate that I should follow him.

The bartender leads us to the back of the bar.

"Wait, we can't have them back here." The first bartender exclaimed.

The other bartender gave the first bartender a look, and he shut up and continued working. The other bartender smiled at us as he turned his attention to us. We were directed to the back of the building, where the kitchen was located. There are two metal doors on the opposite wall from us. There were two signs, one saying exit and the other saying employees only. After walking toward the employees only, the bartender flipped the sign, which now reads, 'Ye Shelter'. The bartender opened the door. This led to a long hallway filled with five doors on each side. Usually, this would lead to a large refrigerator, right?" Ezra asked.

Nodding, the bartender pointed to the doors, "The doors with signs on them are taken. If possible, please take only one room for the two of you. There are not that many left."

As Ezra nodded, the bartender closed the door behind us. He was right; there were only two doors left. There is one towards the end on the right side and one in the middle on the left side. As Ezra looked at me, he asked, "Which one would you like?"

As we walked towards the door, I said, "The one in the middle."

Each door displays a different animal. "When you place your

hand on the doorknob, the signs on the door will display your family's animal." Before touching the doorknob, Ezra looked at me. "Do you want to?"

I shook my head, "No, not that many members of my family are still alive. Therefore, they may be suspicious."

Ezra nodded, "That's true and not many families have a crow as their family crest." He placed his hand on the handle as he opened it. A sign appeared; it was a wolf. The two of us entered the room together.

The room was set up as a studio, similar to a cabin in Renee's pocket universe. However, this room possessed a distinct 1980s flair. The floor is made up of dark wood, the rug is patterned, and the furniture does not match one another or the rug. However, the curtains matched the bed comforter. In the bed/living room area, the walls were burnt orange. There was a lot of lemon yellow in the kitchen area. There were tiled walls in the kitchen area, some with floral patterns. Ezra looked back at me as I looked at him. The two of us began to laugh together. "This is a hot mess. Why would anyone find this interesting?" I asked.

Ezra shrugged, "This is the 1990s. This place has always been a decade behind." Walking over to the bed, he sat down. As he looked at me, he asked, "When would you like to return to school?"

"Should we just take care of it now?" I asked as I started to mess with my necklace, but I realised it was still in the box.

Ezra stood up and walked toward me. As he touched my cheek, he said, "It's up to you, Cleo. My role is merely to provide support."

I rested my head more into his hand, "I think I just want to go, find Mortimer, and get home."

74

Ezra nodded, "Ok, then let's go."

18. Grandmother, What Large Teeth You Have

During this period, Knight-Thorn Academy was not equipped with a protective barrier. Security was lacking before the attack on my family when I was a child. Since the uniform codes were not as strict, Ezra and I could fit in if we wore something from the 1990s. As Ezra guided me to the library, we pushed the large double doors leading to the library. My eyes were drawn to the difference; I was used to seeing computers in the library. Several years passed before my mother, the headmistress, brought computers to the school. She told me that she was paranoid about students using them.

"I'll go this way, and you'll go that way." Ezra pointed in the direction I should take.

"Surely, it did not change that much so that the books would have moved." I responded.

"Estrid said it did." Ezra said, "So, we will split up." I nodded and headed in the direction he pointed. I was drawn to the Dark Matter Magick and Cursed Families category.

I apologise, but do I know you?" A woman asked. I kept looking because I did not believe she was speaking to me. "Hello? Are you deaf, young crow?"

Young crow?

Slowly, I turned around to see Lady Esme Knight, the woman standing with my dad when I was running away. When my grandma caught me, I felt my heart drop. My throat was drying up as I said, "Uh, no. I recently moved here."

"I know I don't have that much family left, so, once again, I ask. Who are you?" Esme narrowed her eyes as she said, "Blood recognises blood, young crow."

"My name is Cleo Martin." I replied.

"Martin? That is a hunter family, isn't it? Please explain why a pureblood Knight vampire would be with them?" Esme asked.

"I'm not sure; I was adopted and then sent to this school." I replied. Technically, this is not a lie.

"Come with me." Esme said, about to grab my hand.

"No, I will not be," I replied. "I have a project to complete for class." I pulled away from her.

"What project are you working on?"

"About Mortimer."

As Esme reached for me, I used my strength to push her away. As she fell to the ground, she looked up at me and gasped, "You are not who you claim to be. Surely you are one of Sebastian's remaining children; I thought you all had died decades ago. Why do you still appear to be so young?"

Sure, we can go with that.

"It is true that I am. I would appreciate it if you did not disclose this information to anyone. You should know what I am capable of." I narrowed my eyes in response.

"If you are here, he needs to know about you. He believes you have all died." She continued, "And if you are still alive, he may no longer stay here."

As I shook my head, I replied, "No, he needs to stay here with Elizabeth. That is the path he should follow."

She seemed confused, "I didn't know any of you could see the future."

My shoulders shrugged, and I said, "Things are best kept secret. Now, I would leave if I were you."

She started to get up, and her eyes closed, "I don't think your dad did a great job teaching you manners."

"I do not believe your parents did." I replied. "You would be a member of the younger generation of the Knight bloodline, would you not? Did you forget that you are not his biological mother?" I sucked a deep breath in. It was difficult to do this to my grandma, but I desperately needed her to leave me alone.

She narrowed her eyes and clenched her jaw. As she opened her eyes, I noticed a powerful 'you-fucked-with-the-wrong-one look'. Blood dripped from her fingertips as she whipped it toward me. I ducked, just barely avoiding it. The blood whip had sliced through the bookcase. As I stared wide-eyed at her, she smiled. "It's all talk and no action; what's the point? Wasn't it my understanding that you were Sebastian Knight's daughter?"

As I stood up, I stared at her intently. As my grip tightened on her mind, she screamed and fell to the ground. More attention was paid to it than to the falling bookcase. Esme whipped her blood again, and my mind just barely stopped it. She was still lying on the ground in pain as I walked closer to her. I whispered to her, "Please stop." I touched her hand as a flash of memory flashed before my eyes.

She was seated next to my mum when she was a child. They were in some kind of formal living room. As my mum cried softly, "Why does my brother not like me?"

"Mum…" I said softly, approaching the couch.

In both the memory and real life, Esme snapped her head towards me, "Did you say, 'mum'?" She asked.

My hand jerked away from her as I gasped and stepped backwards. I tripped on my own feet, losing my balance.

I heard you scream, Lady Esme." Estrid said as she approached Esme's side. As Ezra helped me up, he was next to me. Estrid narrowed her eyes at me. "Do you not realise that she is a pureblood vampire? How dare you!"

"Estrid, please stop." Esme looked back at me and said, "You are not who you say you are; you are a Knight."

"My name is Cleo Martin. I was adopted as a child. Technically, I did not lie." I replied.

Estrid stared at her in confusion. "She is a Knight? What does that mean?"

"Estrid, you should speak to the librarian about fixing the bookcase. I must speak with these two alone."

Ezra was not making eye contact with me as I looked at him. In response, I looked back at Esme.

"Let's go." I replied.

19. Esme Knight

We went to the royal meeting room. It was decorated in the same manner as it is in the present. The fact that it remained the same was a pleasant surprise. The two of you are not from this time period, are you?" As soon as she closed the door, Esme began to speak.

Ezra replied, "No, we are not. We need to locate text regarding who has been associated with Mortimer. We must bring Mortimer back with us. When everything happened, we were searching for the book." He muttered the last sentence.

I sat on the other side of the couch from Ezra. First of all, Lady Cleo shouldn't have come. What were you thinking?"

"Estrid stated that she had seen us in the past. I had to come. Otherwise, things would change in our time. Additionally, only I am capable of handling Mortimer, I mean with the help of the heir." I responded.

Esme appeared confused, "Why would a pureblood vampire be involved in triblood matters?"

I shrugged, "I can't tell you much since it will mess with the future."

Esme nodded, "Ok... Well, I will help you with your task if you tell me one thing?"

"Sure, tell me what it is."

"Do you and I enjoy a close relationship?" Esme asked me.

Looking at Ezra, I noticed he was not looking at me. "I have not lived with the Knight family for most of my life." However, if I were to live with them, we would have a good relationship."

Esme looked down momentarily and thought, "You know there was a prophecy concerning our family?"

After raising my eyebrows, I placed a hand on my neck, forgetting I did not have my necklace. "What is the prophecy?"

"The Knight of Light, under the darkness of the new moon, will end the threat of the world. And the Knight of Void, during the light of the full moon, will end the world we cherish." Ezra stated, "Everyone is aware of it."

Esme shook her head, "There's more to it." She paused, "The Knight of Light, under the darkness of the new moon, will end the threat of the world. And the Knight of Void, during the light of the full moon, will end the world we cherish. The Protector of Death and Time will meet the Knight of Void on a blue moon. The Bringer of Death will meet the Knight of Light on the night of the blood moon. Forever bonded together on the night the sky falls."

Ezra appeared confused, "The Protector of Death and the Bringer of Death wasn't in any of the books."

"Taking a deep breath, Esme said, "It will remain that way." She touched my shoulder and said, "Your father promised me he could not have children, but I guess he lied again." She said, "At all costs, you must stop your father from destroying the world. You must be the Knight of Light and save the world we cherish.."

As I stepped back, her arm fell to her side, "You have the wrong Knight. Once I stop Mortimer, I will never fight again. I do not wish to lead that life."

As she swallowed, I heard her say, "I hope you have a sibling." She turned to look at the painting behind her. I almost thought the painting could have been of my dad, mum, brother, and me. However, I knew it was not the case. "I know Elizabeth wanted twins when she was a child."

"Lady Esme, do you have the book about Mortimer Marcellus?" I took a deep breath, avoiding the conversation about my family.

"Yes, I do. It is in this private library." There was a crow detail at the bottom of the frame that held the painting. Esme pressed the crow as if it were a button. A hidden library was revealed when the painting was flung open. It was not an extensive library, but it had four bookcases about the height of an average person. It would have been very dark for a human, but there was a perfect amount of light in the room for a vampire. To a human, this entire school appears dim.

Ezra and I walked around the bookcases in search of the right book. "There were many books about this island. It was your grandfather's library, my husband's, and he collected many books about the island, Staros, and the small islands surrounding it. Did you know that the school is located on our property? The main building was our family home, but we had to donate it while on the run from Kolby, the bastard son of my and my husband's mum."

Bastard children are the offspring of a pureblood who has slept with noble blood, whether they have a mate or not. If a pureblood slept with another pureblood, the child would still be considered part of the pureblood family.

As I turned my attention to her, I said, "Wait, didn't you say Kolby was a bastard? Why can he hold his own against my dad if he was?"

Laughing, Esme said, "Kolby cannot hold his own with the original vampire, especially not with your dad. Did you know that your dad is the one who forced Selene to give us this cursed gift?"

I looked wide-eyed at Ezra. Ezra had frozen just as he was about to pick up a book. My father did not make the deal; it had to have been another Knight family member who did.

"Young Crow, why did you look at him in such a manner?" Esme asked.

While looking at Ezra, I said, "I had a dream about it; it began a couple of weeks ago."

"Lady Esme, the librarian, has repaired the bookcase." Estrid announced.

Looking at them, Estrid narrowed her eyes as she looked at me. Estrid reminded me of a loyal cat who hated everyone except its owner.

"I appreciate your help, Estrid. I need more time with these strangers. Would you mind leaving, dear?" Esme asked sweetly.

She nodded and left just as quickly as she had arrived.

"What was your dream about?" Esme asked, walking towards us.

"Someone asked Dad if he would like to be damned for the rest of his life, and he agreed. In a flash, I could no longer see him but Selene, the goddess that created vampires. She points behind me," I glance at Ezra, "I see him lying in the lake. While running towards him, I could hear a man talking, but his words were too fragmented to understand."

Esme thought deeply, "The prophecy may be in the works now; you might not have a choice if you want to fight. You have a bond with Selene."

83

I shook my head, "What do you mean a bond with Selene? How could anyone have a bond with a goddess? And I told you, I am not fighting after this."

As quickly as she had appeared, Esme placed a hand on my shoulder, "Members of the Knight family already have a faint bond with the goddess due to his choice. Whenever the Guardians instruct us to fight, we must comply; it is the price we pay for. Something must have changed since only Guardians can see the Guardian's original form."

"Who are the Guardians?" Ezra and I questioned.

"Our makers are not called gods and goddesses, as many would have you believe."

"If they are not called gods and goddesses, then why do we call them that?" asked Ezra.

"It changed one year ago. And it just stayed. I would assume it is because that is what humans call their makers, so to avoid attracting too much attention to ourselves, we copied the humans."

Taking out a book, Ezra flipped through it, "Hey, Cleo, I found the book about Mortimer. The host appears to be Theo MacCarthy. We could use my resources to locate him." He put the book back and walked towards me. "Let's go, so we can return home." He extended his hand to me so I could grasp it.

Looking back at Esme, I said, "It was a pleasure meeting you. I hope that we will meet again."

Esme nodded in agreement.

20. Our First True Date

"**A**re you not planning on erasing your grandmother's memory?" Ezra asked as we returned to Woemi.

I took a deep breath; I did not look at him. "My grandma dies in a couple of days. Now that I know, I travel back in time. I assume that it is related to this mission. And why Cass knows about this mission."

"Several supernaturals wanted the Knightleys to investigate your grandmother's death but refused. The Knightleys used their ties with Lady Clarrisa to ban further talks about Lady Emse's death before changing of the Fae Courts. I forgot your grandma died of unknown causes."

After Ezra guided us to Grim Goat, I waited at the front door for him while he went to the bar. In a whisper, Ezra spoke to the bartender, who listened attentively. My gaze was drawn to the bar. I had not taken the time to look around the bar during my last two visits.

It had a rustic, almost old feel to it. It was all made of dark wood and a decent-sized fireplace left of the bar. There was a single six-top in front of the fireplace. Several people were drinking over there. They were pretty loud, the only ones in the bar besides me and Ezra. There was a girl not much younger than myself who caught my attention. She had lavender hair, similar to-

As the girl turned towards me, her appearance changed. Her appearance now resembled that of Ronnie. I blinked a couple of times.

"Ok, time to go." Ezra told me he was in front of me. Looking around him, I could not see the girl at all. Ezra stared at me confusedly, looking in the same direction as I was.

"Sorry, I must be stressed out." I turned my attention back to him, "I thought I saw Ronnie."

Ezra touched my cheek, "I want to show you a place."

I nodded, "But did you get someone to get more information about Theo?"

Ezra smiled, "Yes, now we get to enjoy ourselves."

We proceeded towards the centre of Woemi. Woemi looks the same as it does now; a few stores have been updated, but only a few. There has always been an old feel to Woemi. Inquiring about his destination, "Where will we be going?" I asked, grabbing Ezra's hand.

Looking back, he smiled, "I have wanted to take you to this restaurant since we first arrived at Cypress Institute. However, I have never had the chance."

My smile spread across my face as I replied, "Ok, let's go."

We arrived at the restaurant, Crow's Keep. The restaurant had food for vampires, but each supernatural creature was represented by at least one dish. We got seated fairly quickly since they were not very busy. "Whatever you want, my treat," said Ezra, sitting on the other side of the two-person table.

I looked at the menu, "I want to order the extra rare."

The waiter smiled, "A woman with excellent taste! And for you, sir?" He turned towards Ezra.

"I will also have the extra rare." Ezra handed the waiter our menus.

"I will prepare them for you." The waiter dashed away.

I looked at Ezra, who was staring at me. "Do I have anything on my face?" I asked as I placed a hand on my cheek.

"It is nice that we can now do couple things again. We have not been able to do that since everything started. It is nice not to worry about guilt or being too busy to do things like this."

As I placed my hand on him, I smiled. "It is nice. Once this is over, we will have to do it more often." I said.

In a flash, the waiter brought the still-beating hearts to our table. Going from human meals to things still moving on my plate is strange. "Enjoy your meal, and let me know if there is anything I can assist you with." The waiter disappeared.

As soon as I picked up the heart, I began to bite into it. "You certainly have something on your face," Ezra chuckled.

21. The Pulled of Desire

The two of us walked hand in hand to our safe house. We are fortunate that no one has sought us out. As I took a deep breath, I realised I should stop worrying about things like that and enjoy the time I spend with Ezra while we await information about Theo MacCathy.

As I relaxed, I turned suddenly to Ezra, who had closed the door to our room. As I rushed to him, I slammed him against the door. Even though he was taller than me, I pinned his hands as high as I could above his shoulders. I could feel the slight sparks of our bond, but they have not been as strong as before. Spending more time with your soulmate strengthens the bond you share. The more you become one instead of two separate entities. As I gently pressed my lips against his, I could feel he was trying to take control, so I allowed him to do so. As he pressed me against the wall next to the door, I let go of his hands so we could let our hands roam. I gilded my hands around the back of his neck while his hands traced down my body to my legs. He helped lift me so my legs were around his waist. He started to walk us. "Where are we going?" I giggled as I held on to him.

He plopped me down on the bed; my limbs were still wrapped around him. I tried to keep every part of him as close to me as possible. As his mouth moved down to my neck, I gasped. Taking a few breaths, he paused there. "Are you okay?" I asked, pulling his face to look at mine. Now, his eyes were a deep red colour.

It used to scare me so much when I was a hunter, but now I am not afraid of those eyes.

I placed my sharp nail on my neck, gently pressing it against my skin. His eyes grew brighter as I guided his head back toward my neck. Ezra whispered, "Are you sure? It is more than just us having sex. Blood sharing is a sacred bond between mates."

Since vampires do not receive nutrients from other vampires, sharing blood was sacred.

"Aren't we mates?" I asked as I placed my hands in his hair to draw him closer to me.

I felt him take a few more breaths before he bit down gently. I gasped as a chill went through my body. I moved my hands down to the bottom of his shirt and began to lift it. As he pulled me up to sit on top of him, he kissed my shoulders and neck. Occasionally, he would lick my bare skin, sending sparks throughout my body.

Disappointed, I attempted to remove his shirt by placing my hand under it. As I was about to remove my shirt, he grabbed my hands and stopped me, "I don't feel comfortable taking off my shirt; I have a scar I am not comfortable with."

I felt my heart drop, "From the attack? It did not heal?" I started to try to take it off again.

Again, he stopped me and said, "Cleo."

As I leaned back on the bed, I apologized and pulled him close. We both moved up on the bed as I said, "I'm just worried about you."

"Don't worry about it. Just let me remove my shirt when I'm ready, okay?" He asked, and I nodded.

Putting his hand on my cheek, he pulled me close to his lips. I began to feel the passion again as I kissed my way down to his neck and bit down harder than I intended.

Under my fingertips, I felt his goosebumps, and I smiled as I continued to drink in the essence of Ezra. He tasted amazing; the best drug one could get. No, it is better than the best drug. My brain started the hum with dopamine. Despite my reluctance, I gently pulled my mouth away. I did not want to take all of him at the risk of losing him. If a pureblood were to kill someone this way, they could become overpowered and go insane.

A sigh escaped my lips. In response, he chuckled, "I felt the same way."

Both of us smiled as we made eye contact.

"You have something on your face." His voice is soft as if he is holding something made of glass. He wiped the remnants of blood from the corner of my mouth. When I grabbed his finger to lick the blood, Ezra stopped being gentle.

His lips collided with mine. He entangles his hands in my hair and pulls me up. By moving his legs, he placed me on top of him. I put my hands on his cheeks as we continued to kiss. I moved his head away from me as I kissed down his jawline, down to his neck, till I got to the collar of his shirt. Then I moved my body down so that I could get his pants off.

I asked him, "Would you mind moving your shirt up a little so I can take your pants off?"

He nodded but seemed to hesitate; lifting it just a little bit made it easier for me to get to his pants. After unbuttoning them, I removed them.

It dawned on me that I had never done this before; I was going along with the flow.

"Are you all right, Cleo?" Ezra asked, confused.

"Yes." I replied, "I had never gotten this far with a man. It has never been this close before."

His hand was placed under my chin, and he pulled me close to him as he placed soft kisses on my lips and around my face. "Neither do I." He said softly.

He began to remove my dress from me. Giving me random kisses on my body places not touched by another individual. My entire body shivered as a result of it.

Upon returning to the top, he guided me back down. Our bodies guided themselves wherever they wanted to go, and eventually, I pulled him closer to me. "You remind me of the moon; my night would be a hell of a lot darker without you." I whispered as we grew closer.

As I laced our fingers together, I lay on his chest, looking up at him. "I am glad we had time to ourselves." I responded, "I hope we have more nights like this in the future."

It was a smile on his face, but something else was in his eyes. "I hope so too. Let's get some sleep before our informant arrives."

22. Briar Doppelganger

Ezra woke me up, moving around in bed. This was my first time sharing a bed with someone. I have had sleepovers, but we usually use cots or sleeping bags. Just as I was about to turn over, I heard a soft knock on the door. I put on one of Ezra's shirts and looked through the peephole. The redheaded child looked to both sides of the hallway to ensure no one else was present.

The informant must be this individual.

As I open the door, I say, "Hello."

"Cleo," he handed me a maroon folder, "This is all the information I have about Theo MacCathy. I have important information to share with you."

I took the folder and asked, "Did you manage to locate him?"

The boy nodded, "This is the information I need to share with you." I gestured for him to enter, standing in front of the bed so he did not see Ezra completely. "Mr MacCathy is leaving Scotland tonight at Dock C. He and many other supernatural families are boarding a red-eyed boat as we speak."

"OK, I'll get ready now," I got him out the door, "Thank you again. It was quite helpful."

As if it were a light trick, the kid nodded and disappeared.

Looking back at Ezra, I smiled. Should I wake him up?

Walking towards the bed, I gently shook him. However, he did not awaken. "Ezra. He has found Theo, would you like to go? We do not have that much time left."

As he turned over, Ezra murmured, "No."

As soon as I changed, I rushed towards Dock C. Dock C is located in Woemi, and the docks are the only means of entry and exit for those who do not prefer to portal to the island. Generally, Dock C is only used for shipments, not for travel.

The closer I got to the waterfront, the more clearly I could hear people talking. "You should have taken our offer, Rory. That way, your family wouldn't suffer." A male voice said.

"You will never be king. Someone will always stand in your way! Your family is cursed to never obtain what they desire." another man commented.

The woman chuckled, "Don't you know? We have found a way to break the curse. All we need is the Briar doppelganger."

"Such a thing does not exist." said another woman. "The Briar lineage has been extinct for centuries."

I worked my way up the building to get a better view of everything. My only concern was Theo; I did not care about anything else. There were two groups of people, three on one side of the open area and five on the other. "A doppelganger is merely a myth," The other man said; he had black hair and eyes.

"But, Rory." The man clicks his teeth, "There's one right behind you." This man also had salt and pepper hair and black eyes. Although the two men did not appear to be alike, the younger one next to the older one seemed to be almost identical to him. They could be father and son. The girl beside the son reached out for his hand, but he resisted. Her eyes are icy blue, and her hair is light blonde.

The other man, Rory, looks behind him; I look at the four people behind him. My jaw nearly dropped to the floor, as I had been viewing things before. She resembled Ronnie almost exactly, but she had a scar above her left eyebrow, and her mannerisms differed. She still had hazel eyes and brown hair. Theo was next to her; he had hazel eyes, but they were more on the yellow side, and he had dark brown hair.

"We have found the key to breaking the Valentine Curse and finally defeating those bloody Knights once and for all." The man stated.

"You have lost your mind, Vincent," Rory shook his head, "the doppelgangers do not exist."

He shook his head and said, "See, Rory, you were wrong. That girl, that doppelganger, has visited our town so many times. However, no one seems to note how far apart those times are. Every 35 years, that girl comes to this island like clockwork."

The boy on Vincent's side began to walk towards the other group. Rory stepped before the boy in response and said, "No, Victor. I think you should keep away from my family if you know what is best for you. Your daddy still has some influence over the council to get you off with a slap on the wrist."

Victor raised his hands. Victor looked at the girl beside Rory and said, "Listen, old man. I only did what your daughter has been begging me to do since we arrived on this island." His beady eyes turned a soft, glowing red. "Isn't that correct, Thea?"

She glanced away and mumbled, "I didn't want to."

He scoffed, "Oh, yeah, Dad's here now. Go ahead and act all innocent."

A woman who looked similar to Thea stepped in front of

95

her, lifted Thea's chin, and said, "Listen, sweetheart, we believe you even if no one else does. We are here now, and we will protect you."

A lady stepped out of the dark, and with a snap of her fingers, the white candle in her hands lit up. She had short dark hair and soft blue eyes. They are working with a witch. Pulling Theo out by myself might be more challenging, after all. Vincent said, "We don't want your daughter, Dorothea. We want the doppelganger, Violet, but if you get in our way, we will do everything in our power to stop you."

"Don't forget the boy." A familiar voice shouted from the darkness. As I listened to his voice, I felt almost numb.

Mortimer.

23. Aeonian

Of course, he would be here and know where Theo is. He wore his usual suit and slicked back his hair. He appeared exactly as he did in my mind.

He stammered, "How are you out in the real world? I thought you were sent to the Martins on the main island."

Mortimer did not respond to him, keeping his attention focused on Vincent. "I informed you of the location of the doppelganger, and your promise was for me to retrieve the child."

As Vincent side-eyed Mortimer, he replied, "You are *just* a triblood, and you should be aware of how tribloods are treated."

There was a look of anger on Mortimer's face.

Vincent shrugged, "But since he seems important, I may want to take him with me."

Mortimer shook his head and began to walk towards the other group. "I just want the boy; he has something I am interested in."

Victor grabbed Mortimer's upper arm, "No, triblood. That boy belongs to us now; you cannot possess him." Victor used his vampiric strength to push Mortimer against the wall of the building I was on top of.

"Okay, Rory, here are your options. You can change into a

human the easy way or the hard way." Vincent growled.

Rory shook his head, "Why? We did nothing to you."

In a wicked smile, Vincent replied, "Yet, you have not yet. However, you will be an obstacle when we break this curse and attempt to retake the throne from those bloody Knights. It is impossible for anyone to get the throne technically. Due to our limited influence over the world compared to you and the Knight's families, the Valentines must be the last pureblood family to hold the throne."

Does this family have any claim to the throne? Keeping them from turning human would allow me to avoid taking over the throne.

Likely, they are still human in my timeline.

But...

"What about the Grimwalds? They could take your throne from you." Dorothea asked.

Vincent shook his head, "The Grimwalds are too passive to take any action. They no longer want the throne and are willing to give it to us."

Victor scoffed, "More like too weak to fight." Turning to Rory, Victor said, "So, old man, give us an answer."

Grabbing her dad's wrist, Thea said, "Da, let's just go easy. We can start the new life that we have been wanting."

Rory looked at Dorothea for a few seconds, making eye contact with her. Dorothea nodded, "We will remain together."

"In actuality, you and Rory cannot remain together. Soul-mates can break the Human Curse; we cannot have that happen while attempting to stabilize the world. However, we are not complete monsters. One of you can remain with the liar, Thea." Vincent replied.

Dorothea glanced at Rory once more. As they nodded,

Dorothea raised her hand and pushed Vincent, Victor, and the young girl into the portal that Dorothea had made. Vincent shouted, "Ethelred!" The witch with them set up an invisible net to catch the three. They were still being pulled or pushed into the portal that Dorothea opened. Ethelred began to chant a spell. As my heart sank, I realised that it was the Human spell.

As much as I do not want to interfere, I would also like to know if this family could be the key to not having to take the throne. I should intervene. In addition, I am still determining how this decision will affect the world in which I live.

I was jolted out of my thoughts by the group's screams of pain. Shit, the spell is affecting Theo. It is a bad thing for Theo to be human. He would be defenceless. However, if I jump down there, the spell will also affect me. Mortimer groaned, was he also affected by the spell? Peeking down, he rubbed his head as he attempted to stand up. He yelled, "Ethelred! What are you doing? You can't use her for the spell if you turn her human!"

"If she stops, Dorothea will keep this portal open." Victor shouted.

Vincent muttered, "Shit." After thinking for a moment, he came up with an idea. I am not sure what changed in Rory, but something changed. Rory held a knife to Thea's throat. "Now, Dorothea, stop the portal, or the first thing you will do as a human family will be to kill one another."

She glanced at her husband and daughter. "If Ethelred continues, she must stop doing one of her spells. She cannot continue performing both spells at the same time." Rory told his wife.

Thea began to cry, "It hurts, stop."

Dorothea glanced at her family and then back at Vicent and his family.

"Dorothy, don't do it. He will kill us either way and does not care if we live or die." Rory exclaimed.

"Dorothy," Vincent mocked, "You just need to stop the portal; then, you and your family can become humans and be on your way."

Dorothea let out a sigh, and the portal vanished. Vincent began to laugh, "You dumb cunt!"

I turned my attention back to the father and daughter. I used my powers to push the girl away, and she fell to the ground with only a superficial injury to her left shoulder. Then Vincent said, "No matter." Rory punched himself in the chest, causing his heart to be removed. As soon as he held it in his hands, it turned into glowing ash. His body followed shortly after that.

As Dorothea and Thea ran towards where Rory was, Dorothea screamed at Vincent, "What have you done?"

Vincent shrugged, "That way, you will not be able to recall who you are. I will not have to worry about you trying to claim the throne. You and that lying bitch will have to live their lives as human beings."

"But I stopped the portal as you requested." Dorothea sobbed.

"It's a punishment for both of you. You for trying to fight us, and Thea for lying that my son touched her without her consent." Vincent explained.

The other two, Theo and Violet, fell to the ground due to the pain caused by the human spell. "Ethelred, you can stop the human spell. At least until I can remove Violet and Theo." Vincent said.

I had to get in there now that the spell had been stopped.

As I jumped down, I landed directly in front of Vincent.

"I assure you that this has nothing to do with you." Vincent replied.

"Ah, hello there, Cleo." Mortimer said. "I see that you figured out who I bonded with back then. You arrived just in time."

As I snapped my neck toward Mortimer, I declared, "I am not speaking with you. You are why I cannot live a normal life."

Mortimer scoffs and smirks, "Isn't all this action normal for someone of Knight blood?"

My eyes narrowed as I looked at Mortimer.

"A Knight! How is that possible?" Victor asked, "Sebastian and Elizabeth don't have any kids."

"Who said that I was Elizabeth's or Sebastian's child?" I asked as I looked at the Valentine family. Looking within myself, I pulled on the ashy blue string.

24. Faction of Power

"What is wrong with her?" Victor inquired.

"This is a woman of Knight blood, for sure. Those bastards traded their souls for a darker, older form of magick." Ethelred said.

Vincent looked at her confusedly, "Darker and older?"

"Magick of Dark Matter." Ethelred said, taking a few steps backwards.

Vincent looked back at me and replied, "She's just a kid; how much damage can she cause?"

"I cannot control her." Victor muttered in fear.

I felt a slight pull, but nothing too severe. The dark energy gathered into a ball as I held out my hand. It grew and grew until it reached the size of a basketball. There was a sense of dark energy taking over me. When I released it into the sky, lighting fell around us. It hit whoever it wanted, and they all tried to flee, but I did not allow them to leave the open area. With this murderous lightning crashing around them, they were all trapped here.

It was almost as if I had been holding onto a weight that only now began to dissipate. The feeling of freedom was overwhelming.

I felt-

Right before Ezra bit me, I felt relief from everything happening around me.

Ezra.

As I touched my neck, I felt the weight build once more.

The weight was me pulling the Dark Matter Magick back towards me.

As I looked around, everyone was lying still on the ground. My heart sank; I had no intention of killing anyone...

It became increasingly difficult for me to breathe the air around me. I was out of breath, and my knees could no longer support me. There was a build-up of tears in my eyes. What have I done?

Standing here, I am in awe of how easily my abilities have controlled me. I may be becoming a Level E vampire. Those are the vampires that fail to convert from human to vampire or pureblood vampires that drain the last drop of blood from a living being.

I heard a groan behind me; I turned to see Thea move slightly. In a hurry, I approached her and said, "I am so sorry. I should not have travelled until my power was under control."

Thea said, tearing up, "My parents. Are they ok?" They started to get up. Thea crawled over to her mother, whispering, "Ma."

Dorothea touched Thea's cheek. Dorothea smiled at her daughter. "Hello, sweets. I'm sorry I wasn't strong enough to save him." Her voice cracked and weak.

Thea shook her head, "No, mama, it's not your fault. It's Valentine; it's always them."

Dorothea looked at me, "You should not be alive. You should have died from using so much power."

Mortimer said, his voice filled with excitement as he started to get up, "She barely scratched the surface of what her dad could accomplish." He smiled wickedly, "You're just like me, after all."

I shook my head, "I would never be anything like you!" I shouted.

"Well, princess, I'm afraid you do not have much choice with the road you are on." Mortimer was next to Vincent's body on his side and pulled a white sword from his body. Vinceant's body became ash as it floated in the wind. Mortimer turned his attention back to Ethelred, who was barely getting off the ground, saying, "Let's go, Ethelred."

"You cannot control me, triblood." Ethelred hissed.

Mortimer scoffed and held the sword tightly in his hands. Then he turned to Victor and the other girl and said, "Let's take them with us and transform them into humans." And she created a portal for them to travel through, which appeared below the entire group. Mortimer smirked at me as they sank through the portal. Screaming stopped me from running after them to finish Mortimer.

"No, Ma! It is over, do not leave." I turned back to see Dorothy transforming into glowing ash, like tiny stars returning to the night sky. Thea was screaming and crying at her mother. Violet began to get up and walk towards Thea to comfort her. Violet stopped me from walking further. "You have done enough."

I stopped in my tracks and nodded in agreement. "I apologise."

24. FACTION OF POWER

25. Some Wounds Never Heal

I plopped on my stomach on the bed. It was a long night, and I did not even have a chance to speak with Theo. I placed my hand on Ezra's cheek. He had rolled to his side, so I joined him in bed.

As I lifted the blankets, I noticed his shirt was slightly raised. There was a red patch on the side of his stomach. Getting on my knees, I lifted his shirt higher. A shifter scratch on his side had become infected. His veins, as well as the skin around his wound, were green.

In response to my shaking Ezra more, he quickly got up. As he panicked, he asked, "What happened? Are you okay?"

"I thought you said you had fully recovered. Why did you come if you were still injured? Why didn't you tell me?"

"I don't know…" Ezra replied, looking away. "I just wanted to be ready when you wanted to leave. I didn't want to be the reason we did not leave when we did." Ezra glanced up at me. "Look, Cleo, I'm sorry." He reached for me, and I stepped back, getting off the bed.

"I'm worried, Ezra. What if your coming here makes my dream come true?" I asked, blinking quickly to stop the tears from falling.

As Ezra said, "I know you'll save the day if anything goes

wrong. After all, your dad is an original vampire, after all." I looked back at him. A gentle smile spread across his face.

"The problem is that I have been a human for years, Ezra. I do not have complete control over my powers yet. How can you trust me to save you?"

"I know you possess a great deal of power within you. Your power intrigues me even now. Once you have a proper education with someone who can control Dark Matter Magick, you can do much more. We know only your father and Mortimer have access to the old magick, and your father is deceased, and Mortimer is in good health…."

"And I have something to confess as well." I blurted out, "You cannot tell anyone, and you cannot get mad, do you promise?"

Ezra nodded, "I promise. It's only fair, considering I hid something from you."

"My parents are not dead. They are in a stone sleep in the old animal building. Estrid was also in stone sleep, but something happened that caused her spell to wear off. We are not certain what happened." I replied.

The silence was so thick I almost couldn't breathe.

Your brother told me when he was an assistant teacher that I had to do everything I could to find his sister and bring her back to the school so the spell on Estrid could be removed. Your brother said you had to go on a special mission, but he never informed me." Ezra said. "Once I saw Estrid again, I knew. Estrid even confirmed, but she requested that I not inform you."

I am glad she told you that. If Kolby had known my parents were still alive, their entire plan would have been ruined. Were they discussing this particular one? I mean, it had to have been…" I murmured. As I looked into his dark eyes, he appeared to be relaxed. There is no longer any pain hidden within his eyes. As I touched his cheek, I said, "We are partners, bonded by many bonds by now. We cannot hide anything from each other, okay?"

He nodded and placed his hand over mine on his cheek. "No secrets." He smiled as he moved to kiss my hand. "How did it go last night?"

Last night?

Looking out the window, I noticed that the sun was beginning to rise.

I placed my forehead on his, "The short version is that Theo is safe at the school. The school knows who he is because of Esme, and Mortimer has a powerful witch with him who changed the Valentines into humans. I have learned that Ronnie is part of a doppelganger line that the Valentines need to break their curse. And I may have changed the past… by letting the Giannes go without turning into humans. At least I do not have to take the throne."

As Ezra sighed, he said, "I knew you couldn't help yourself. At least this way, we can live a quiet life after this."

I replied, leaning closer to kiss him, "Yes, we can. In the same way as last night."

A smile spread across Ezra's face. "Oh? What's your favourite? Maybe we can end with that?"

I shrugged and smiled, saying, "The whole night was my favourite part."

It began as a gentle kiss, but it soon became something heavier. As he guided us back onto the bed, I wrapped my arms around him. My tripping caused us both to fall over onto the bed. We laughed as we took off our clothes and collided with one another. "Are you sure you want to foul around with your side hurting like that?" I asked, propping myself up with my elbows.

As he drove straight for my neck, Ezra kissed up my neck and then down to my breast. Between kisses, Ezra murmured, "I'll let you know if I need to stop."

Nodding, I sank back into the bed. As I guided him back to me, I placed my hands in his curly hair. As I pulled his neck to my mouth, I gently bit down on it. I took some of his blood for myself. He gasped and pulled away from me as he kissed me and returned to my neck. "Now, it is my turn." He bit harder than I did. Even though it did not hurt, I felt a cool sensation travelling through my body. It is almost as if you were diving into a swimming pool on a hot summer day. I enjoyed how good it felt. As he continued to bite down, I moaned. It was as if my essence was being transferred from my body to his. Just before the coolness became too cold, he released me and licked my blood. When I flipped us over, I pulled his body close to mine. He pulled me back to his lips as I kissed his body just before I got too far down. "We do not have to go that far if you are uncomfortable with it." he said as we stared into each other's eyes. "Are you?"

I shook my head. He nodded, pulling my head to his, and we kissed passionately.

26. The Invitations

When we got up, there was a knock at the door. As soon as I got up, I opened the door. A deep blue letter was lying on the floor before the door. When I went to pick it up, I noticed it was sealed with the school's seal.

"What's out there?" Ezra was behind me.

As I displayed the letter to him, I stated, "It is from the school. Should I open it? Do you think they have the wrong door?"

Ezra shook his head and said, "I don't think they got the wrong door. Open it." He guided me back inside as he closed the door behind us. I began to open it. Gold words on the dark blue paper glowed brightly whenever the light was directed at the right angle.

THE ROYAL BALL
JOIN US AS WE CELEBRATE THE COMING TOGETHER OF
KNIGHT-THORN ACADEMY.
22TH OCT. 1989
7 PM

"It's an invitation to the royal ball. I didn't know Knight-Thorn had those; I thought it was just a Cypress thing?" I said, showing him the invite.

"Even The Knight Academy had them, though the humans

from the day class thought it was a party with other humans from the night class. How mistaken they were..."

"Wait, my grandma dies the same night as the party..." I realised. The showdown would be the final act, wouldn't it?"

Ezra placed his arms around me without saying anything. The two of us eventually pulled away from each other, and I was about to put the invitation on the kitchen counter when words in silver ink appeared as the gold ones disappeared. "What is that?" I asked while picking it up.

I initially noticed nothing on the paper until I turned to face Ezra. There was a glow emanating from the invisible letters on the paper. The letter stated the following in silver words:

Meet for a vampire-only party

20 Oct. 1989

8 PM

{please bring invitation}

I looked up at Ezra after reading it aloud. It may not be a good idea for us to go. We have already had several close encounters."

"Well," Ezra replied, "we could always go to town and find enchanted masks. Masks are generally worn at Cypress parties. In that case, no one will recognise you, and we will have no further problems. The party is tomorrow, so we have to get some masks all day today."

"I'm not sure, Ezra. Is there even a mask strong enough to block the blood recognition thing?"

Ezra shrugged, "I'm sure there's something. I suggest we ask Renee, but those bracelets do not work."

I looked at my wrist, "I don't have my bracelet anymore... I probably lost it last night or my fight with Esme."

Ezra nodded, "We will have to figure this out alone. I can

search for an enchantment mask, while you can search for Valentines or Gainnes since you know what they look like."

"Why should I go look for them?" I asked, confused.

"To ensure that they are removed from this island. The council would have discovered them already if they had been on this island at present." Ezra said as he approached the closet. Thankfully, this place leaves donated clothes for people who don't have anything. He wore clothing that appeared to be from the 1980s, with shoulder pads built into every part of the garment. He pulled out a sweater with many different colours on it and some jeans.

"But now the Valentines are human. So, I doubt anyone would know what the Valentines looked like." I replied, following his lead. I picked something pretty much the same, but the sweater looked different.

"I just want to be on the safe side. As he finished getting ready, Ezra said, "We don't know if we can even trust anyone."

"I will go and see if I can find the Valentines. They should have been aboard the first ship to leave this island today." I started as I finished preparing myself.

27. The Last Encounter

I visited the place where I last saw the Gainnes and Valentines. A man's voice said, "You won't find who you're looking for, princess."

As I turned to see Mortimer, I was surprised to see him. His appearance was different, almost as if he was fatigued.

I asked, annoyed. "Why did you do that?"

A smirk spread across Mortimer's face. "What?" he asked. "I assumed you would be pleased to see me. It was I who brought you home, as you are aware. If you had not done this, you would not have been able to see your parents or brother again." He began to walk towards me.

We were in a large space, and many people passed by us. The people around us were moving around us rather than bumping into us.

"My parents have passed away. What are you talking about?" I asked, making sure he thought I was clueless.

As Mortimer approached, he said, "Oh, I might have heard from your uncle, who heard from a little birdie who saw you talking to your parents. If the council finds out you are hiding your parents, they will curse you for remaining human."

"It is a good thing I was unaware of their existence." As I stepped closer to Mortimer, "I wondered if you were fooled again."

Mortimer's smirk fell, "Listen, princess, I just want Theo. If you give him to me, you will never have to see me again."

"How did Theo become your host? Theo had been a human until you bonded with him."

"Well, unlike you, he was not a human. In addition, unlike you, he reunited me with my bloodline. Perhaps he is smarter than a pureblood. How ironic! I have always believed that purebloods are the most intelligent people."

"Well, I had been a human and a hunter, neither of which are known for their intelligence," I explained. "If you have nothing to add, I have a family to look for."

"You will not be able to locate them, Cleo." Mortimer said softly. Before I could ask, he had already responded, "If they ever became human, the Valentines had a plan. This is their ultimate revenge on you, your family, and the Gainnes. There are great things to be said about their revenge, and you are unaware of it since you are stuck in the past." Mortimer smiled.

"Weren't you the one who changed them into humans? How could they have taken over the present?" I asked.

He shrugged and said, "I may have piggybacked off of the plan and told them I had helped them become vampires again. This did not sit well with them." He walked toward me, touching my hair with his fingers. He forced me to look up at him. His face was inches away from mine. "You, princess, changed everything when you intervened to prevent the Gainnes from becoming human. You scared that witch so badly that she wanted to help me, and the Valentines stopped you."

I was about to speak, but he disappeared.

Shit. I need to find Ezra and tell him what has happened.

I started rushing back into town without knowing where I

was going. I began to panic; this was all my fault once again. Everything I touch, everything I do, I ruin.

When I stopped running, I gazed up at the fountain in town. At the top of the fountain, it resembled the angel at the school. Unlike the other, this one reached down while the other stood upright.

As I fell to my knees, I held my head. I am overwhelmed by everything that happened since people discovered that I had Mortimer in my head.

I looked back at the angel who was reaching down at me.

"Some believe that Selene watches over this island, and the fountains you can find everywhere with the angel serve as a reminder of this." As she sat at the fountain, a girl said in a familiar voice, "You will never be closer to Selene."

Violet.

"I would like to thank you for saving my life. While it may not have seemed like it, I was comforting my friend. The majority of Purebloods do not interfere with the affairs of others. In light of this, I wanted to reach out to you and thank you for getting me into that fancy school." Violet adds, "I understand I am just a lowly shifter with no ties to Selene. It may also be out of line to say this, but I consider you my Selene."

As I smiled, I softly said, "Thank you. Sometimes I wish she would come down and take away my gift. There are times when I wish to be human or even…dead."

Violet tilted her head.

The way she acted was nothing like Ronnie, but they shared the same face.

"Why would a pureblood want to give their gift away?" She inquired.

Looking down, I said, "I have been tasked with so many

things; I do not wish to fight anyone else's battles anymore. All I do is ruin everything."

Violet touched my shoulder; I didn't feel a flash of memory. I looked at her, confused, which caused her to pull away. "Oh, I'm sorry, princess. I overstepped!" Violet stuttered. She didn't make eye contact with me.

I never saw memories with Ronnie either...

Could it be a doppelganger phenomenon?

"No, it's just- I don't know why but I can't see any of your memories. I see flashes every time I touch someone, but not with you."

Violet turned to me and said, "Well, that makes sense. Most abilities do not affect me. As a pureblood, I am confident you could do it if you tried hard." Violet laughed nervously.

"Is that the Brair doppelganger's ability?" I asked, getting up.

Violet shrugged, "There isn't much over the Brair doppelganger, so that I wouldn't know."

"Do you feel comfortable if I tried to see a memory?" Sitting beside her, I said, "You may say no."

"Uh, I mean, you may try. But even Lord Sebastian and Lady Elizabeth did not see anything." Violet said, "And they belong to the oldest pureblood family, the Knights."

I chuckled, "Yeah?" As I reached out my hand, she placed her hand in mine.

When I closed my eyes, I felt an ashy blue string inside me, which kept me focused. By focusing my power on one flow, I can maintain control.

The ashy blue string led me to a river and a meadow surrounding the river. Both appeared to go on forever in both directions. A sun could be seen in one order, and a moon could be seen in another. As I walked towards the river, I could see her recent memories, such as what had happened yesterday. It would be helpful to see the first memory, as it may lead me to her ancestors. My father once discussed a theory regarding how the doppelganger was created. The strongest Knight can possibly see an ancestor's ancestry. Even though he was the strongest, he could not accomplish the task.

However, he is not me.

There is no control over me, no direction for me. As a child, I never followed the rules regarding my abilities. Instead, I did what I wanted. I began running toward the moon. It is in the darkness that we begin.

Something hard struck me, causing me to fly backwards.

"None of your kind here!" I heard a female yell.

28. Bonnie Briar

"Who's there?" I asked as I started to get up. In the midst of the darkness, I was unable to see anything. I began to walk toward whatever I had just hit.

"You are the reason." The female continued to yell with a thick old Scottish accent. "It is entirely your fault."

"What are you talking about?" I asked. "You do not sound like Violet at all. Could you please tell me who you are?"

"I am the one who will get my revenge. I will bring her back and end your kindness!"

The voice was becoming louder. "I want to help." I said, still reaching out.

She scoffed, "Like a vampire could help. You bring nothing but destruction to the world."

"Yeah, honestly," I replied. "I would like to correct that about myself; I do not wish to keep ruining things."

"Like you ruined her?" The female replied softly.

There was a flash of colour and light, almost like I had been thrown into a portal. However, it did not feel like a portal. I was at the lake with the meadow nearby. This time, however, there was an old town on one side and a forest on the other. I know this place; this was one of the other towns on Staros.

Kilus is that town, and only a few people live there in present. Kilus is used by students who cannot or do not wish to reside at Cypress.

There was a couple on the grass next to the river; it was the Briar doppelganger and a girl I didn't know. She had brown hair and brown eyes. The girl kissed the doppelganger on the cheeks. "I will love you forever, Celeste." said the doppelganger.

Celeste pulled a knife from her dress pocket and sliced open her palm. "Then, let's promise." Celeste replied. "I know we are already mates, but you know what would happen if the town found out about us."

Bonnie, the doppelganger, smiled and extended her hand. We should make a blood pact."

I felt the world flip; now it was night. From the forest, I could hear screaming. "He waited until she was alone; he knew she had not yet activated her abilities." I turned to the voice.

Celeste gazed into the river. She had her hood down. "He knew he wouldn't get into trouble since she was still considered human." Celeste commented, "She killed herself when she discovered she was with child."

The town and forest disappeared into the sun and moon again. Moon is the town, and the forest is the sun. "I tried everything I could to bring her back. Unfortunately, I could only obtain a doppelganger, so I cursed the Valentine bloodline. In other words, the Valentine men will not reach Vance's age when he did that to Bonnie." Celeste glanced at me. "I gave the doppelganger protection against most supernatural abilities.

"Due to the curse I placed on the Valentines, the doppelgangers will always appear. Their blood will continue to maintain balance, a way for the Valentines to break their curse."

Celeste paused and glanced away, "There must be a connection between you and the doppelgangers. They seem drawn to you."

"My best friend is a doppelganger. I am sure she thinks I am some psycho by now." I said, looking down at my feet.

"There is still a connection; the doppelganger did not cut it. You should speak with her again and maintain that connection." Celeste commented, "Doppelgangers are powerful anomalies, and it is a blessing to have them by your side. You also have a great connection with your ancestors to be able to talk to someone dead for as long as you have. You are a very powerful individual, aren't you? No, this is something unique about you. Another power within you."

Violet pulled her hand away from me, ripping me away from the place I was at, "Are you hungry or something?"

As I looked at her confusedly, I replied, "No. I had something to eat last night."

"Well, your eyes have been bright amber for a while now. Did you find anything?"

"If I am being honest, I have found everything. The key to breaking the Valentine's curse lies in you; as long as the curse remains in place, the Doppelgangers will continue to appear." I replied, standing up. "I need to find someone. Thank you very much, Violet, for everything." I began to walk away. I needed to find Ezra. I think I have a plan to stop Mortimer.

29. Vampires Everywhere

Ezra was back at the safe house. "I believe I have found a way to stop Mortimer," I said, excitedly walking into the room. "A method that does not require Celine's bloodline. Since Mortimer has to die in the past, and no one at this time knows which bloodline is the strongest to Celine."

Ezra smiled, but it was weaker than usual. "Oh, yeah? How are you going to do that?" He asked.

"Ezra, are you okay?" I asked, walking closer. I sat next to him on the bed.

"The pills are no longer effective. As each day passes, I feel weaker and weaker. I have less energy to do anything." Ezra said, not looking at me but at the floor.

"We can help you by using the blood of a doppelganger. The blood is supposed to cancel out the effects." I said as I rubbed his back with my hand.

He laid his head on my shoulder and asked, "Do you wish to risk changing the present?"

As I rested my head on him, I said, "I am afraid I may have done so already. I saw Mortimer; he said that my uncle had told him about my parents and that the Valentines had already taken over the present. And that they are waiting for me to get back."

Ezra took a shallow breath in and then exhaled. "I still believe that we should not attempt to do anything else. It is just a matter of eating regularly and being careful not to overdo it."

"Okay." I replied softly. "Did you find the masks?"

"Yes," Ezra replied softly. "I have placed them on the table. Would you like to rest with me before we leave?"

As I helped him to bed, I nodded. As I wrapped myself around him, I allowed him to rest on my breast. "Save all of your strength, okay?"

While snuggling back into me, he kissed the back of my neck.

I lay there contemplating how I would locate Violet. No matter what, I will not lose Ezra, no matter how difficult it may be. My dream needs to come true. No matter what I must do, I am willing to do it. There will be peace for me, damn it.

We started getting ready, and he wore a wolf mask as I wore a plague doctor's. In addition to my spaghetti strap red silk dress, I wore black gloves and sheer black lace over the dress. The red blazer that Ezra wore was matched with the slacks and black shirt that he wore under it.

When we entered the party, no one turned to look at us. All vampires wore masks, not delicate-looking but those made from dead animals' bones. Service personnel wore delicate-looking masks with various patterns and a black button-up shirt with black slacks. Even for a supernatural being, the lighting was dim, almost as if the candlelight had ceased to burn. My eyes were much more comfortable when everything was always so bright.

There was haunting and ethereal string music playing; most vampires were dancing, but some were standing and drinking from a glass filled with blood. Some individuals drank directly from the source, wait staff or blood donors, in corners.

We almost appeared to be invisible until Esme noticed us. She wore a mask resembling a crow skull, "I didn't recognize you. That was a clever idea to get enchanted masks, though you look somewhat out of place." Esme said, "I have added Theo to the servicing staff so you can speak with him. I would have asked him myself, but I did not know what you needed to ask." She pointed to a man wearing a delicate mask with lace patterns, "There's Theo." Theo appeared to be wearing a tuxedo.

"Thank you so much for pointing him out." I said. I was about to walk there when Esme grabbed my arm and stopped me.

Esme whispered, "I would wait until later in the evening when everyone is drunk. Everyone will notice if a server leaves without providing them with their drinks."

I nodded, "You're right."

"So, have a good time. There is something for everyone." She winked at us as she walked away.

I watched as she began talking with someone...Dad? I turned quickly away, looking down.

As Ezra rested his hand on my upper arm, he said, "Cleo, it's okay. He will not notice us if we do not pay too much attention to ourselves."

I looked up at Ezra, "But Esme could still find us...So, he might be able to as well."

As Ezra shook his head, he pulled out the invitation. "That is why she said to bring the invitation so that she can even find us." I looked at him, confused, and he held the invitation toward me. "Take a whiff."

Leaning in, I began to smell an unhealthy human, which smelled like overbearing perfume. As I turned away from it, I said, "Oh, it is not strong unless-"

"It is what you are looking for. Which is how Lady Esme found us."

I nodded, "That does make sense." I looked around but did not make eye contact with any Knights. In this time period, the Knights would have been on the royal court; at least Esme would be now that she is not running. Her daughter, my mum, would be running the school under the last name Knightley. As I stared at the ballroom dancing vampires, I glanced at Ezra, who had not noticed my gaze. "Let's go dancing." Ezra looked uncertain, "Come on, please." I gently nudged him with my elbow, "Esme said we should fit in." I smiled.

As a new song, Nocturne No. 2, began to play, Ezra held out his hand and said, "My lady, may I have this dance?"

30. Dark Chocolate

As we exited the dance floor, both of us were laughing. "I had no idea you had those kinds of moves, Ezra."

Ezra shrugged, "Well, maybe we can go again?" He raised an eyebrow.

"Yes, of course. Let me get a drink first; I am thirsty." I replied.

"Okay, then I'll go have a seat somewhere. I'm getting exhausted." Ezra began to walk away. Grabbing his arm, I turned him toward me.

"Are you all right? Is it your wound?"

"Yes and no. I haven't danced long, so I'm also out of shape." Ezra said, then he touched my cheek, "I would let you know if I wasn't doing well because of my wound, okay? No more secrets, right?" I nodded as I placed my hand on his. He kissed me, "Okay, then I will have a seat." Ezra gave me a soft smile before navigating the crowd. As Ezra moved through the crowd, I watched him briefly.

Although I feel bad that he came, if he had not come, I would probably have lost control over my powers at least twice now because of how stressed I am, mainly because I have to wait for everyone to be too drunk to notice anything. I turned to walk towards the refreshments. "What would you like tonight, miss?" the bartender asked.

"Well, what do you have that won't make me drunk? I am the DD." I replied.

"Um, we do just have blood, if you want that? However, most everything contains alcohol." he replied.

"I would like to take A positive then. Would you happen to have dark chocolate?" I asked.

The only human food that supernaturals would be willing to consume is dark chocolate. As the darkness increases, the more enjoyable it becomes.

"Yes, we do." He placed a small bar of dark chocolate before me, and I began eating it. "An excellent choice. "I'll get some real quick." He replied, walking to the back of the bar. Behind him was a door. In a blink of an eye, he handed me a clear wine glass filled with red liquid. "There you go, miss." I smiled and thanked him. As I turned around, I bumped into someone.

With a gasp, I held my head down. I do not know who I bumped into, but they have a strong pureblood aura around them. I cannot believe that I failed to notice them until just now. "Please accept my sincere apologies. I am unsure what got into me today, but I have felt a little lightheaded." I looked up and noticed I had spilt my drink on him. "Oh, I am deeply sorry."

I looked utterly up at him.

Dad.

My heart began to beat rapidly. I was only met with cold eyes staring back at me. I started to back up because I was pretty close to him. He used to be a stay-out-of-my-personal-space type of person. He was the more lively of my parents when I was a child. My mother was always working because the school required most of her attention. When she was not working, she was fully dedicated to my brother. When she retired, she wanted him to take over the school. As a child, my father was the only one with me unless he was on a business trip, in which case Estrid watched me.

He narrowed his eyes and asked, "Who are you?" Asking the lady beside him, "Did you invite her?"

The woman was not wearing a dress like ladies wore back then, but off-white pants and a dark green shirt or coat like a gentleman. The woman shook her head but paused, "You know, she does look familiar to me. Was she not invited by Lady Esme or Lady Elizabeth, Lord Sebastian?" Her dirty blonde hair was braided in an updo.

Estrid behaved very carefree as a child when she was with me and my dad. This contrasts the present and the past, where she has been much more careful and proper.

There was no response from Sebastian; he was looking at me intently.

She narrowed her hazel eyes and asked, "Are you related to the Knights in some way?"

My mind wandered momentarily, and I was unsure how to respond. "I was adopted, I do not think I am, my family is a smaller noble family." Which isn't a lie; I was adopted by Crystal, my human mum.

"Oh, have you ever met your parents?" She replied.

"If I did, I was young and had just awoken from a human spell." I shrugged.

"Is that why you don't look good?" she asked, looking at me more closely.

Sebastian whispered coldly, "Estrid." Sebastian continued in a low voice, "You've just met her; things are different here than in the Fae world."

Estrid gave a nod, and she looked back at me, "Sorry. There was no ill intention on my part when I said those words. I just say whatever is on my mind."

"It's okay." I replied.

"What are you? The mask makes it hard to tell." Estrid asked.

"I am only a noble."

Sebastian narrowed his eyes and asked, "Which family?"

"The Thanatos." I replied, throwing out a random noble family name. The Thanatos mainly lived in America, and not much pull anywhere, a lower-ranking noble family.

There was a pause.

"Okay." Sebastian replied. Then he leaned close to me, just barely touching my hand. He was worming his way into my mind. In my mind, I grabbed the ashy blue string and pulled it away from him, preventing him from it. "Light blue…" He whispered in my mind, staring at me for a long time. There was a dim red flash in his eyes.

"Did you see anything, Lord Sebastian?" Estrid inquired.

"Yes. She's okay; leave her be." Sebastian lied as they walked away.

31. The Blood Ties

I shook my head and said, "I think we should leave. Perhaps we should declare the mission a failure and go into hiding. Just me and you. There is no need to worry about the rest of the world."

A confused Ezra asked, "What? Why?"

"Sebastian bumped into me. I told him I was a noble but thought he would be on to us soon. I tried my best to lie. I pulled my string in a way that helped me control my powers, and he had seen the colour before I could conceal it. He lied to Estrid, but he will still be on to us. My dad never stops."

"What colour is your string?"

"It is an ashy blue colour. The same as my mum's."

As Ezra gazed at the ground, he said, "Well, you have said that he lied to Estrid. No one in the Knight family leaves Estrid out of things, as she is the best tracker in the family. Even better than shifters and the whole supernatural community. So, hopefully, we can finish what we need to do tonight. We can then go find Mortimer and go home." Ezra got up and walked towards me, brushing my hair away from my face. "It will all work out in the end."

"And yet I have a gut feeling that it won't be okay."

"The plus side is you stopped having those dreams."

Looking down, I said, "But even Esme believes the dream will come true. I mean, part of it already had occurred with my father accepting the gift from Selene."

As he lifted my face, he said, "If you continue to say that everything will go wrong, everything will go wrong. You must think positively."

"It's hard when I'm surrounded by pain and torture."

Ezra kissed my forehead. "Please work on it for me, okay?" I nodded. "Okay, let's go inside and see if we can speak with Theo."

We returned inside and searched for Theo. However, many people were in this room, making it impossible to locate anyone. "Should we separate?"

Previously, the band was a vampire band, but now it was a fae band. "That's odd."

Ezra nodded, "Maybe it would be best if we didn't split."

"Why?"

"For anyone not in a good headspace, this music is similar to a bad trip on any drug. It is especially harmful to mortals." Ezra paused, "What if your father does this?"

I shrugged, "Maybe, but let's just find Theo and get out of here."

"Let me know if you feel strange," Ezra thought, narrowing his eyes. "We will leave and get away from everyone." He said, "You must promise me you will let me know."

I nodded, "No more secrets."

"Okay, good. Now let's find Theo so we can leave."

There was a strange air in the crowd the deeper we got into it. Ezra regularly checked on me to ensure I was not losing my mind. Thankfully, not. It felt like I was in an aeroplane, or at least that is how it was described. My human mum had been on a plane before.

The deeper we went into the crowd, the less lit it became. We were both in the dark. Fortunately, we had our supernatural vision, so it was not too serious. "Do you know where you are going?" I inquired.

In response, Ezra shrugged, "No, but the music will keep everyone on the dancefloor. They do this bit at the end."

"So, does all Fae music control the mind?" I asked.

Ezra shook his head and replied, "No, but most of it does. This is how they select the weakest candidates."

"Pick the weakest?"

He nodded, "Yes, back when Fae discovered they could play music like this. Because the human tribes surrounding the supernatural tribes believed that the supernatural tribes were monsters and deserved death, the Fae assisted the tribes by locating their weakest members. The tribes sent out their weakest member to the humans, making them believe they had destroyed all monsters. We have created barriers and worlds to keep humans away from our worlds. The higher-ups still celebrate the Day of Remembrance as a form of remembrance to show their gratitude to those who died. The holiday is Nilulenn." He grabbed my upper arm, "Let's leave now."

"Why? I asked, looking at him with confusion. There was a subtle change in his facial expression and body language.

"Remember how I mentioned that some higher-ups still celebrate the holiday?"

I nodded, "Yeah."

"It will take place tonight." After midnight, most humans will die; the Fae bands begin to play at eleven o'clock. We have an hour to find Theo."

"Will be dead? It was the weaker supernaturals, right?" I

asked. My heart was pounding if any blood got near me. My control would probably be lost entirely.

"Yes, but the higher-ups use humans to protect supernaturals and sacrifice them to those who have died." He replied, and we turned around. Since he was right, I did not put up much of a fight.

"Lady Thanatos." I heard a voice call out.

32. Hellfire

I turned to see my dad, and he was with Theo...

As Sebastian walked towards us, he said, "Ah, I thought that was you." The crowd parted to accommodate him. As a result, we are all in an open circle. "If I understand your request correctly, you want to meet with this young man." His voice was so chilling, and he spoke slowly, but not so slowly, that it was difficult to focus. He seemed to be paying close attention to every word he said. His eyes would be the only light a mortal would see. It was as if he had hellfire in his eyes.

As Ezra stepped back, he put me behind him.

Sebastian appeared confused, "I am not here to harm you... I thought you would leave if I gave you this triblood. Should you refuse to leave, I will personally throw you out."

I stepped past Ezra, "You won't be able to hold him off, Ezra."

"Oh? Do you believe you are capable of handling an original?" There was almost a laugh in his voice.

My eyes were fixed on him, and I nodded in agreement. "We would leave the school if we obtained this individual."

A soft smile spread across his face as he passed me, "Is he someone important to you?" He was now standing next to Ezra. I could sense Ezra becoming tense under the pressure Sebastian purposefully exerted upon Ezra.

As I placed myself between them, I said, "Yes, he is my mate. We will leave; just let us have Theo."

He looked back at me, "Answer me truthfully, and I will give you this, Theo."

"Fine, what is your question?"

"Who are you? You and your friend are not affected by the music. Therefore, it is evident that you are not noble." Sebastian asked; he narrowed his eyes, "You must be of pure blood."

I reached for my mask.

"Cleo, no." Ezra said.

Then I glanced at Ezra and said, "Let's just get this over with. It is likely that he already knows."

Ezra looked towards the ground but nodded, "He probably does."

Both of us removed our masks.

Sebastian's eyes were no longer glowing. As he stared, he did not say anything.

Before anyone else notices, I put my mask back on. People like my mum. "Time travel. The future is in trouble, and I am responsible for saving it." I paused, "Please give me Theo."

Sebastian asked, "What does this triblood do with anything?"

I shook my head and said, "You and Esme already know too much. However, both of you are blocking our progress."

Although I hated being rude to him, there was no time to spare.

Nodding, he let Theo go. He rushed to me, "Hate to be in the middle of two purebloods, but I would rather go with the stronger one." He muttered.

Sebastian narrowed his eyes and glanced behind us. I turned to see a man as he approached us. He was wearing a cloak.

Could he be a wonderer? The guard said, "Sir, you cannot be back here."

The man apologised, "Sorry, I must have wandered too far." He turned around, wearing a mask. His scent, however, was that of a familiar forest. Even if I tried, I could not forget.

Mortimer.

As I turned my body to face this man, I grabbed Ezra and Theo by their arms, holding them too tightly. I placed them both between myself and Sebastian. Hopefully, I am just imagining him.

As the man began to walk towards us, he stumbled over himself. Mortimer and that man must have shared the same smell. Most supernaturals share the same base scent; then their deodorant, body soap, and anything else they use to make themselves smell better will add layers to the smell. If someone does not care for themselves, that also contributes to the layer of smells that constitute that individual's scent. As he walked away from us, and eventually, when I no longer smelled him, I began to relax. I let go of both Theo and Ezra.

"Can we get the information we came for, please?" Ezra asked Theo.

Theo asked, confused. "What information?"

"All the information you have about Mortimer. How did you unbound from him? Is there anyone else he bonded with?" Ezra continued to ask questions

My attention was focused on the man who had walked past us. Making sure he does not return.

Then I heard Theo ask, "Do you lose control sometimes?"

As I looked back at him, I nodded in agreement.

"I think because we bonded with Mortimer, he somehow takes some of our power to be stored with his. We are users of

Dark Matter Magick." Theo stated. "I am not as good at Dark Matter Magick as you are."

I thought it might have been me missing my brother, but maybe Mortimer did take a piece of me with him. There has always been something off about me, as if I could never enjoy life fully. I feel as if I am wearing this mask even when I am with Ezra.

"She can't bond with Mortimer. She would have had to+" Sebastian started.

"Be human. Yeah, no thanks to you and mum." I finished.

As Sebastian looked down, he said, "I apologize. If we had known-"

"Both of you knew. It was you who had told Cassius about this mission."

"You have a brother."

I nodded.

He smiled, "Your mum always wanted twins."

Once again, I nodded.

As Theo leaned towards me, he said, "You could tell it was him, didn't you?"

I asked, "How were you able to tell?"

"This scar will burn when he is close to me," Theo said, showing his right cheek. "I didn't think I'd have to worry about him again."

Mortimer was that man...

33. Promises to Another Lifetime

While looking around for him, I asked, "Where did that man go?" The man disappeared so quickly.

"What, man? Is that why you pulled us behind you?" Ezra questioned.

"Yes, that man was Mortimer. "I do not understand how he managed to get into this party since it is a vampire party." I looked around, but I could not detect him. If Theo had not mentioned it, I would have thought I had imagined him.

Suddenly, everything began to move slowly.

When I turned back to look at Theo, I saw Mortimer coming from behind and attempting to stab him with a sword. I threw Theo behind me using my vampiric speed and reflexes. Nevertheless, they were not fast enough to prevent Ezra from jumping before me and blocking the sword.

"Ezra!" I screamed, trying to pull him away from Mortimer's blade.

I wasn't fast enough.

As I rushed to Ezra, he was already lying on the ground in great pain. It was the exact location of the previous wound. Blood was oozing from his injury, "Ezra, what were you thinking?" I asked, panicking. I kept the pressure on the wound, but his wound was not healing. "You're not healing." I held myself as close as I could.

Ezra was gasping in pain as he looked down at his wound, as I held him in my arms. "Cleo," he said softly.

I shook my head, "No, save your energy."

"When death takes my hand, I will hold you with the other and promise to find you in every lifetime."

I shook my head again as tears fell on his cheek. "Ezra, it's not supposed to end this way."

Slowly, he raised his hand and wiped my tears away. He smiled softly and said, "We will find each other again."

"Ezra, I cannot live without you. How am I going to find my way out of this darkness without-" Mortimer interrupted me.

In a smile, Mortimer said, "Kolby told me where Janet had already attacked him. I had to make sure I had a means of stopping you, Princess."

Everyone started to rush outside. The Knight family and a few members of the school staff remained.

"It's too bad you couldn't save your lover." Mortimer leaned toward me, "No one will be on your side regarding our fight."

I heard thuds all around me. When I turned around, everyone except Theo and I was awake. Gently, I placed Ezra on the ground and quickly stood up.

Mortimer looked up at Theo while Mortimer was starting to get up, "You were right about me taking a piece of you when we bonded. It's why I had to ensure you and Cleo didn't fall asleep. Otherwise, I would as well."

My gaze returned to Ezra as I brushed his curly hair out of his face. My forehead touched his as I said, "I'm sorry I got you into this mess."

"Now, Princess, I know you spoke with Celine. Tell me how to break this curse, and then maybe I will be able to enlist the assistance of my new witch friend to assist in this situation." He gestured towards Ezra.

I shook my head and said, "I will not tell you. I will never tell you."

Mortimer made a nod as he looked at Ethelred. Mortimer grabbed Ezra, and I attempted to pull him back to me, but in a flash, Mortimer and Ezra had disappeared.

In a state of panic, I searched everywhere. "Ezra!" I screamed, searching everywhere for him.

A hand grabbed my arm, "Cleo, he's not here. Mortimer and that witch took him."

I turned to see Theo and said, "No, there was no portal." I shoved Theo off me and looked around. "Ezra!" I yelled as I ran through the gardens. "Ezra, where are you?"

"Cleo, it's pointless to look for him." Theo said, keeping up with me. For a hunter, this is quite shocking.

Looking at him in confusion, I asked, "How can you keep up with me?"

He shrugged, "I'm not sure. It happened the night I met you."

"That's strange. Yes, hunters are part vampires but generally found in lower ranks…" I thought out loud. Unless Mortimer is not the only one who gains a part of us, could we also share details of the different hosts? It is also necessary for us to identify Mortimer's weakness if I am to stop him and secure Ezra's return."

He crossed his arms and said, "I'm not sure. There's no way to know if that's how it works. It's not like we can talk to The White Witch."

"Who is the White Witch?"

"Well, Celine, of course."

Why is she known as the White Witch? Is it because she can

perform Light Matter Magick?"

"But, like I said, there's no way to talk to her. She died a thousand years ago."

"There is a way." I said softly.

34. The White Witch of Crystal Blue Lake

"How can a pureblood vampire talk to the dead? Are you a devil?" Theo asked as he followed me down to Crystal Blue Lake.

I shivered when I heard the word devil again. A person I considered family betrayed me, and I nearly died at the place we were headed.

"No, silly. Pureblood vampires cannot be devils." I said as I made my way through the Haunted Forest.

"Then, how can you talk to the White Witch?"

"Her name is Celine, and I'm sure she wouldn't like it if you called her the White Witch."

"You speak with her often?" Theo nearly fell, but I caught him.

"Yes, particularly when I was a child. Knowing that I have been linked to Mortimer, it makes sense that I would be able to contact her."

Theo asked, "So, do you think I could talk to her too?"

I shrugged, continuing to walk, "If you can handle the poisoned waters."

He began to walk again, trying to catch up. "The water is poisoned, and you used to bathe in them as a child!"

I shrugged, "When I was young, I did not know they were poisonous. The singing came from the waters, and I followed it. That is when I first met her."

"I didn't know she was a siren; I thought she was a witch."

"I thought she was a witch," I shrugged. "She did not appear that she was a siren." I continued walking; we were near the lake.

The lake looked just as it did today, really dark. Despite its appearance, it still had a certain amount of flow.

As I approached it, I began to walk into it.

"Are you going in?" a nervous Theo asked.

"You are welcome to stay out here if you wish. It is not my intention to compel you to do anything."

If it had been Ezra, I would have advised him to stay out of the lake, especially given his weakened condition.

I felt a sharp, quick pain in my heart. If I had held on to him, I might have been able to keep him by my side or at least go with him.

I took a deep breath and forced those feelings to the side. Right now, I should focus on stopping Mortimer rather than thinking about him. Preventing any further deaths, at least Ezra is alive. Through the bond, I can sense that much.

As I walked, I glanced at the waters and kept walking until I was pulled underwater by a force.

As I breathed my last breath, I was submerged in water. My eyes were closed until I felt like I was no longer moving.

When I opened my eyes, I saw Celine standing before me. There was a shimmer in her hair that resembled the moon's brightness. Her eyes were the same colour as a clear blue ocean. Unlike the first time I saw her, she was covered in mud. She wore a white dress that was floor length with pearl accessories and pearls on the bottom part of the dress.

She smiled and said, "I see you have become whole again." Her voice was soft and gentle.

I nodded confusedly, "Yes, but this is the past. How could you have known I was not whole?"

In the lake, time does not move in a straight line. Every day up there is the same day down here. Since I last saw you, it has just been a few minutes. After saying this, Celine turned her attention to Theo and said, "Hello, Theo MacCathy."

"How do you know my name? How did I get down here? I wasn't even in the water." Theo exclaimed.

When I brought Cleo down here, I pulled you in. It would be best to have you both present for what I have to say. There are only two days left for you to prepare."

What? Only two?" Theo said, "Wait, that's the ball!"

Celine nodded. "Yes, that is the day Mortimer intends to kill you both. The curse will be broken." Celine paused, "However, you know how to stop it without one of my descendants." Celine raised an eyebrow in response.

As I nodded, I said, "There is a doppelganger. By using her blood, I can stop Mortimer permanently."

Celine nodded and warned, "Be careful with their blood. Their blood is much more addictive than normal blood. It is important to be careful with the person who created them."

"According to her, they are designed to have protective properties." I replied, "So, if I can get one now, I will be protected from any attacks Mortimer may throw while trying to syphon his powers."

"Did you speak with the person responsible for the doppelganger line? Is that possible?" Celine asked.

"Dark Matter Magick and having a strong connection with

that doppelganger line is what I'm guessing."

"Cleo, that's not how it works." Theo said.

I shrugged and replied, "I don't know how anything works. I do things."

"Have you ever had recurring dreams about Selene, the Wishing Guardian of the Moon?" Celine asked, slowly

Looking at her confusedly, I asked, "Why?"

Celine takes a deep breath, "Fate has a lot in store for you, Young Crow."

"Young Crow?" Theo seemed confused. He looked at us back and forth. "You're a Knight Pureblood?! How?"

"Time travel. Keep up, Theo," I said, returning my attention to Celine. "So, is it true about the prophecy? I was hoping Esme was wrong."

Celine nodded, "The prophecy is very much true. However, fate seems to have much more in store for you."

"Is it because my family plays an essential role in the destruction and salvation of the world?"

Celine nodded, "Your journey has only begun, Cleo Knightley."

"I-" I stopped and looked down.

"You simply want a normal life." Celine finished for me. I nodded in agreement. "Most of us who get pulled into plots feel that way. I know I still do; all I want to do is to let go. But if I do," She gestured around us, "all this will leak into the lands and kill everything below. Thus, I must not give up." I felt a hand on my shoulder, "Neither should you. No matter what this wicked life throws at you, it would help if you did not give up. You must keep going."

"But, why me? I didn't want this." I looked up.

Celine shrugged, "Because we have the power and strength

to stop the evils in the world. No one else is capable of doing so. However, you are helping the world from Mortimer."

"What exactly is Mortimer's plan?" Theo asked.

Celine looked at him, "To end all purebloods and nobles."

"I mean, would it be that bad? They are just selfish beings who don't care about anyone but themselves." Theo turned to me, "No offence."

"Our supernatural world would cease to exist if the purebloods stopped existing." Celine sighed. "There would be no new supernatural beings. Eventually, these bloodlines will die out and become human. Human is the more dominant trait when the nobles and purebloods stop existing. We may still have order, but everyone will fight over it, resulting in multiple civil wars. There were major battles for the seats on the Night Court. The Fae world would collapse since the world is interconnected with the four pureblood courts of the Fae. The common Fairfolk can't create new worlds. As a result, more Fairfolk may be noticed and killed by humans, which might lead to the end of the Fae race. Mortimer is also after me, so who will keep the Dark Matter locked away in the lake?"

Theo looked down and said, "I didn't realise how important purebloods and nobles were."

She took a deep breath, then turned to me and said, "Focus on learning how to siphon Dark Matter Magick. By using the Doppelganger blood, your powers should be enhanced as well. You will need more time to learn how to control the blood empowerment that purebloods obtain by completely draining a being. If you can master dark matter syphoning, then you should be in good shape."

Is Dark Matter Syphoning easy to learn? Is there someone in my family who knows how to do this?" I asked.

"He goes by the name Sebastian Knight or perhaps Sebastian Knightley. He was the first pureblood vampire."

"The one who made the deal with Selene? Is he even alive? All the progenitors were sealed away, right?" Theo asked.

I looked at him, "You've met him."

He appeared confused, "I did? When? At the party?"

As I nodded, I said, "Yes, the vampire brought you to me and Ezra. In the future, he will also be my dad."

"What? That bloke have a child? Who could ever love someone so cold?"

"My mum. My father was not cold when he was my father; he was very kind and caring. He was the best dad anyone could have hoped for." I said, recalling all the bedtime stories he read to me.

"No way. I don't believe you." Theo said.

"It's true. I am also his daughter, so I am certain that he was still cold to others." I replied, looking back at Celine. "Is there anything else we need to do to prepare?"

"Focus on dark matter syphoning. Learn how to handle the sword."

"A sword?" Theo asked, confused.

"Yeah, why a sword? I thought Mortimer would be using Ethelred."

Celine sighed, "I cannot say much more than that, or else I will change the future. It's enough that you have already done."

It made me feel guilty since I had almost forgotten about my friends who were in the present. Imagine how the world would have changed n a blink of an eye for them.

As I nodded, I said, "Right... Thank you for all the advice you could provide. I will see you next time."

"Maybe." Celine gently smiled again. "It is possible." An

intense pressure engulfed me, and I had to close my eyes to escape it. Upon opening them, our heads were above water. As we moved towards the shore, we began to make our way along it.

"At least we did not drown," Theo said as we helped each other out of the water.

"See, it wasn't so bad after all." I said, looking him in the eye.

He scoffed, "Yeah, the world will end in two days."

"One day." I said, pointing at the sun.

"Oh, that's great. One day." Theo said, sighing.

35. And So It Begins…

Upon reaching the top of the hill, Sebastian, Esme, and Estrid were waiting for us. As we made our way up, Esme smiled gently, "Hello, Young Crow." she said. "Hello." I replied.

Estrid began, "How bad did Celine say it was?"

"Well, Celine said, we have until the ball. How did you know that we were going to the lake? And that Celine was there to provide the answers?"

In response, Estrid shrugged, "Well, I can track anyone anywhere." She motioned towards Sebastian, "Lord Sebastian knows Celine is in the lake. As Mortimer and Celine were tied together, we figured Celine would be aware of the situation."

I nodded, still confused, "I will need to learn how to use dark matter syphon. I would also need blood empowerment, but Celine believes it is only possible for me to do both in our limited time. In addition, I should ensure that your memory of me is erased before I depart. While still maintaining the notion that something will happen, but do not clearly understand what it will be."

Esme took a deep breath and asked, "Blood empowerment and dark matter syphoning? I do not even think that I could do Blood Empowerment."

Nodding, I turned to Sebastian, who had not even raised his head to look at us.

Esme turned to Sebastian, "You are the only one capable of using Dark Matter Magick. Could you teach her how to use it?"

Sebastian shook his head, "No."

"Why not?" Esme asked, annoyed.

"I told myself I won't teach it ever again."

"Why?" I asked.

I lost my last child to it. There was no way he could handle the pressure of syphoning just the basic Magic, let alone something older than us." Sebastian said, turning to walk away.

"But I'm not like them." I exclaimed. "In addition to the generations of the Knight Bloodline running through my veins, you are my father as well. I am stronger than them; otherwise, why would fate choose me to fulfil the prophecy."

Sebastian stopped in his tracks, "I won't risk it."

"Then I will practise using the lake. There won't be anyone to guide me." I muttered.

Sebastian appeared before me within a second. "I told you no, and if I must lock you away, I will."

The sight of his hellfire eyes almost caused me to cave in.

"I do not believe you understand." I said my voice low.

"I understand enough."

I shook my head, "No, I saw the look on your face when I pulled my string away from you. I am probably stronger than you, and you do not wish to release the monster I will become. Either you assist me in preventing the world's end, or I will do it alone. I would appreciate your assistance in controlling the beast within so I do not lose control when the time comes."

For some time, he stared at me.

I shook my head and walked away. As I turned around and began walking down to the lake again, I said, "Fine, don't help me."

He muttered, "Fine." When I turned back to him, his eyes were no longer hellfire. "I will assist you. When you reach your limit, you must stop in the real fight. I will finish if necessary."

As I smiled, I asked, "See?" "Was that so difficult?" I slapped him on the upper arm.

Estrid looked a little perplexed.

"It is because I am his daughter, and he knows I am correct." I smirked.

Esme nodded, "I am glad that someone other than Elizabeth influences him." She chuckled. "Let's go inside and investigate how we can assist you with Syphon Magick."

I nodded as they began to walk up the hill towards the school. But I looked up at the stars and prayed that Ezra would be okay. I need him to know what I would do.

36. The Secrets of Knight Manor

Unlike Cypress, the Knights still own most of the main building. Some staff members who have been there for some time might stay at the manor, but only about five of them are there. The remainder of the building is used when the Knight has guests. The decor is the same as it is at present. I have sent Elizabeth away." Sebastian replied, "I do not want her to be involved in this at all."

"I am sure she was not pleased with that." Esme replied.

Sebastian sighed, "No, she was not."

As we turned the corner, we encountered a hallway that led to a dead end, but we continued walking straight. At the dead end, Esme walked closer to the wall. She had removed the family necklace and placed the crow piece on the middle panel of the wall.

"This leads to the fountain outside. The one with the angel." Estrid informed me. It was the same one where Ezra and I hung out. "There is a protective barrier along this path so that magic cannot pass through or out in case of an attack. During Viking attacks on the island, it was also the place where children and wounded were sent. Lady Esme's great-great-grandfather probably prepared these when another tribe of supernaturals attempted to attack the island."

"Oh, really? Why are we heading here?" Theo asked.

Estrid didn't look back at him, "It's so Lady Cleo can practise Dark Matter Magick without hurting anyone else."

"What about us?" Theo asked.

We will be protected from her magic by Lord Sebastian's shield. Hopefully, it will be strong enough." Estrid said.

As we walked down the narrow steps, each creaked as we walked. I felt my heart pounding. If I am unable to do this, what should I do?

Sebastian responded, "If you are a child of mine, you will be able to do it."

Looking at him, I realised that I had spoken it aloud. "I may still be learning the basics. For most of my life, I was a human being."

Everyone was stopped in their tracks by that statement.

"Wait, what?" Estrid blurted out, "What do you mean you were human? Is it possible for you to be human and then turn Pureblood?"

Esme asked, "Lady Clarissa created the Human Curse for those who had betrayed the Night Court. Have you betrayed the Court, Young Crow?"

I shook my head, "No, mum did it to protect me. As a result, I had a perfect life instead of running away from Kolby."

Esme sighed, "I told her never to use it; as a vampire, it takes your life."

I looked at her confused, "My mum was fine when she became stone."

"She became stone after casting that spell? "Esme grabbed my shoulders, "When you get back to the present, you must wake her up, no matter what she says. You must wake her up and ensure she receives assistance when you return. That girl,

I swear. That spell takes something from you each time you use it."

Confused, I looked at her, "Didn't you cast that spell on your mother? What is it that it takes away from you?"

Esme shook her head and sat on some crate boxes. This room reminds me of the basement where my parents' stones are located.

"It takes a part of your essence." Sebastian said quietly.

"Essence?" Theo asked.

"Your life force. It is what gives you the ability to use your ability. Fae have an abundance of essence, allowing them to cast many spells. Then Tribloods have the next highest amount. Then Shifters use it to change into animals. At the bottom are Vampires, well beside humans. Vampires hardly have a use for essence. Yes, we have abilities, but we hardly use them. So, over the years, we have less and less. When essence becomes dangerously low, we can start to die and turn to dust." Estrid explained, "So, if your mum used that spell on you and then became stone for a long time, who knows if she's even alive right now..." Estrid whispered.

"My mother might just be a stoney corpse?" I asked, softly.

Estrid nodded.

First, I placed them in that position, and now I could be responsible for my mum's death.

"No one who knows her told me she may have died." I replied.

"Does anyone know?" Esme asked.

As I shook my head and looked guilty at her, I said, "I cannot tell any of you. Even if I were to erase your memory, you would still retain an inkling of what I have told you."

The room was silent for some time.

"Let's get started before we run out of time." Theo said, breaking the silence.

Esme smiled softly, "Theo, you're right." She turned to Sebastian, who did not say much. "Lord Sebastian, please instruct Cleo. She needs all the assistance she can get."

He wasn't moving; his gaze was fixed on the ground.

"The sooner she completes this mission, the sooner she will be able to check on Elizabeth." Esme explained.

Inhaling deeply, Sebastian closed his eyes.

"Theo, I suggest you move over here before the wind blows you away." Esme advised.

Theo quickly walked over to the location. "Is it true purebloods have more power than us? I mean, I know purebloods have more power than us."

The Knight bloodline is descended from him. As far as vampires are concerned, he is the oldest known. "The others are either dead or asleep in their tombs." Estrid stated.

"So, why is he awake?" Theo asked.

"Lady Esme wanted a son," Sebastian said, eyes fixed on me. When his eyes glowed, they were like hellfire.

There was almost a desire to back down. However, I needed this not only for myself but also for my family members. Before I could return home, I had to defeat Mortimer. Ezra must be saved. After the world has been saved, we can lead peaceful lives.

Taking a deep breath, I braced myself for the impact.

37. Dark Matter Syphoning

Sebastian's Dark Matter Magick forced me to the ground. As a black cloud surrounded me, I was unable to breathe. Every bone in my body felt as if it were being crushed. The dark cloud sounded like a million bees surrounded me, but there were none. It is just a dark cloud. The cloud began as a light fog, but I could not see anything by the end.

Sebastian said, "Focus on your breathing, Cleo." Sebastian's voice seemed to be all around me.

I was unable to breathe. I couldn't see anything around me. I felt as if the pressure of the Dark Matter Magick was crushing me.

"Let her figure it out." I heard someone say. The voices were becoming increasingly hard to distinguish. It all sounded muddled.

As I closed my eyes, my knees buckled under the weight of the pressure. I was on my hands and knees, trying to avoid hitting the ground.

I took one deep breath in. Then, I felt a sense of light, almost as if I were floating. However, I was not.

Slowly, I opened my eyes. Sebastian appeared to be the only one who was not shocked. He always wore a blank expression on his face.

"Wha-What happened?" I asked. "Where did it go?"

"Lord Sebastian called it back." Estrid whispered, "I told him not to... I am glad he did."

Theo quickly helped me up as he walked towards me. "Are you okay?" He seemed frantic.

I nodded, "I think so."

There was still a shakiness in my voice.

Theo assisted me in sitting on some crates where the others were.

It took me a while to realise how badly I was shaking. I glanced at Sebastian, "I-I" I cleared my throat. "I thought I would be able to accomplish it. Why is it so difficult for me to accomplish it?"

He wasn't looking at me, "I knew it was not a good idea."

Esme walked in front of me and placed her hands on mine. "Sweetie, it is okay if you cannot do it immediately. We are indeed purebloods. Even we must begin somewhere. Don't beat yourself up too badly." She smiled gently at me as if I were glass.

I tried to smile back, but I was unable to do so. I did not have the energy to do so. "I would like to give it another try. If I cannot get it this time, I will try to find an alternative."

Esme looked at Sebastian; he looked back at us. He nodded, "Once more."

Esme patted my hands that were on my lap, "You got this, Cleo."

While getting up, I felt lightheaded, but I tried not to let anyone else see me. I stood in the same spot as before. I braced myself as Sebastian sent a Dark Matter Magick cloud towards me. I took a deep breath as it engulfed me.

I gazed within myself and placed my hand on the ashy blue

string. I focused on bringing in the darkness in. Harness the darkness that Sebastian was blasting to me. I can do it. I have to do it. To save Ezra, I had to stop Mortimer. I had to return to the present to keep my friends from the Valentines and Kolby. And to wake up my parents.

I can do it. I need to keep telling myself that. I can't lose focus.

I started to see through the darkness; a thick fog surrounded me. The pounding in my head caused me to place my hand on my head. But I still tried to focus. I began to hear a louder pounding in my head. I can't lose focus; I have to keep fighting. As I yanked harder on the ashy blue string inside of me, I felt something sharp strike my palms. Warm liquid was dripping from my hands. I lifted my hands out in front of me. To become stronger, I must embrace this darkness. I noticed my ashy blue string getting darker as the dark cloud around me slowly disappeared. I noticed that the line inside of me had begun to turn a navy blue colour.

"Come on, Cleo! You can do it." I could hear Theo say.

There was even a blank expression on Sebastian's face. His eyes, however, gave him away.

As the fog cleared, I could finally see the room before me.

The Dark Matter Magick became overwhelming as the blood drained from my body.

38. Saudade

When I awoke, Theo looked down upon me, and something warm was in my mouth. As I gasped, I snapped my upper body up. After wiping my mouth with my hand, I looked down at my hand. It was blood.

Esme touched my shoulder and said, "Cleo, go easy. When was the last time you had a proper meal?"

I shrugged and replied, "I am not sure. Maybe it was a couple of days ago?"

"You decided to undertake an activity that requires a lot of energy?" Esme asked, worried. "It is important to have a proper feed before you try anything similar again, Little Crow. Thank goodness Theo was here and was willing to donate blood."

Looking back at Theo, I said, "Thank you, Theo. I appreciate it."

A soft smile spread across his face, but he said nothing. He began walking towards the seating area where everyone was seated. Estrid was still placed over there, and Sebastian had joined her.

"It would be best if you took precautions. You would have died if you had carried out this action alone." Esme continued.

"I almost did." I mumbled.

Esme sighed and began to assist me, "Little Crow, that's not the point. You must be careful; let's rest for today and get more blood into you. Tomorrow we will have the opportunity to practise more."

Is there a place where we can stay?" Theo inquired.

Esme sighed again. "It will be down in tunnels. I cannot risk Elizabeth finding out about you two. Or about the dangers that could come here."

"Why? Isn't she the headmistress? Why should she not be aware of this information? I asked, leaning against a wall for support. "And where are those tunnels located?" I had thought there were not that many tunnels underneath."

"There is one under the fountain in the gardens." Estrid replied. She would put her life on the line for this school and her students."

"Isn't that her choice?" Theo asked.

Estrid looked towards Sebastian.

He was the one that answered, "I refuse to let her put her life in danger."

"You don't have the right to dictate what she does." I responded.

Estrid leaned towards me, "You don't say no to a progenitor."

"He is first and foremost my father, a family member. Progenitor last." I replied, not taking my eyes off him. "I could always speak freely to him."

"It's not the father, you know." Esme replied.

Standing, I said, "But he will be. I need to rest; I still feel weak."

39. Serein

We went outside to the gardens and were guided through the building's hallways. It was the same gardens that Ezra and I would visit. We headed towards the three-tier fountain with the angel on the top. This was the place where I was awakened. Sebastian hadn't joined us; he wanted to talk to Elizabeth. As a result, Esme, Estrid, Theo and I were the only ones present. While walking to the fountain, Esme whistled the song that my dad used to play on the piano when I was a child. Whenever he returned from a business trip, he would play me this song. These business trips would never be planned; he would always come and go as needed.

In response to Esme's whistle, the fountain's bottom layer lowered and expanded under the ground below, revealing a set of stairs leading downwards. As the water fell down the stairs, it almost resembled a waterfall.

"This school has a lot of hidden secrets, eh?" Theo wondered.

As Esme nodded, she said, "Yes. The Knight Manor has many secrets; it takes years to learn them all." We made our way down the spiralling staircase; it felt as if we were walking for a few minutes before lanterns began illuminating. "The lanterns are enchanted to detect movements." I heard Esme say as she and Estrid stepped to the side to allow Theo and me to see the room.

It was a small house. We entered the first room, which was the formal living room. The walls were painted in a strange blue colour. As I walked around the room, I noticed that the furniture was red and that there was a faint smell of blood. As we walked further into the room, a fireplace lit up automatically. There was an open archway leading to a long hallway. A second archway was located behind the couch. The door led to the informal living room and the kitchen. There was a bar area in the kitchen and a dining room with a large dining table and a smaller dining table.

"This is where Sebastian and Elizabeth were raised, primarily Elizabeth since her cousin was hell-bent on stealing her. It isn't easy to find the underground manor despite being connected to the manor. It's a maze trying to find it." She paused and said, "I could show you your mother's room. I believe you, and she would share the same interests."

As I shrugged, I replied, "I am not sure. I was closer to my father than to my mother. As a mother and brother, we were always in charge of the school; my brother would shadow her. As a result, I was primarily under the care of my father."

Esme nodded, "I'll show you Lord Sebastian's room. There is no doubt that he would not object to your staying there. There was a space between his room and everyone else's. Originally, it was an extra office, but he decided he wanted to be away from everyone."

Estrid told Theo, "And I'll show you to a guest room."

We went our separate ways in the hallway. Theo and Estrid went left, while Esme and I went right. Both sides made a turn; the left side turned right, and the right side turned left.

Sebastian's room was located at the end of the hallway.

"Okay, this is his room." Esme pointed towards a door.

I began to walk towards the door. I asked. "Are you not allowed to enter the room?" I asked.

Esme shook her head, "Sebastian does not want anyone to be in his room. Since you are his daughter, I am sure it should be alright." She smiled softly as she turned to leave. "I will check on you both in the morning. There should be some food and drinks in the kitchen."

"I thought no one lived down here."

Esme nodded, "It's just in case something happens."

It makes me wonder why my parents did not simply come into this room and hide? In place of the stone curse.

When I entered the room, I replied, "Oh, okay, thank you." Except for a desk and a bed, the space was largely empty. Most of the colours were grey, except for the wood, which was dark brown. When I tried to turn on the light, nothing happened. Therefore, the bulb might be damaged. As I made my way to the bed, I sighed.

The room felt significantly colder than the rest of the house despite being underground. However, it was shockingly warmer elsewhere.

My eyes were fixed on the ceiling as I lay on the bed. A silver light illuminated it. As I began to rise, I looked around for the source of the morning. It was almost as if the light was reflecting off of the water. The closet was emitting light.

My attention was drawn to the double doors of the dark wooden closet. Slowly, I pulled on the gold nops. In comparison to the room, they were warmer.

That's strange.

Upon opening both doors, more silver light filled the room.

Warmth was brought to the freezing room by the light. The experience was shocking, almost like jumping into a cold pool on a hot summer day. But it was the opposite.

It took a few blinks for my eyes to adjust to the new light.

There was a sound of water dripping down. I was drawn to a small pond with a small waterfall and began walking toward it. A small amount of lighting emanated from the pond. The sight was breathtaking. It was not just a closet but a mini paradise.

"You have been tempting fate, haven't you?" A ghostly voice spoke. The sound was so faint that I almost missed it.

As I got closer to the water, it became warmer. I began to see clouds reflected in the water.

Standing near the pond, I could see seven silver pillars. Several darker clouds obscured my view of anything else.

Where is this?

Looking around the room, I noticed a hooded figure in the corner. They were on their knees. "Hello? What is this place?" I asked. Their hands were chained above them.

There was no response from the figure.

I approached it and asked, "Hey, are you all right?"

As I removed the hood, I discovered that it was Selene. She appeared paler than in my dream, and the black liquid was coming from her eyes. Selene fell over, causing me to jump back. She had wrinkled skin, and her eyes seemed to be darker. Not so much in colour, but almost as if she was no longer there. "Cleo, you've been gone for far too long." The ghostly voice said. "I will die without you."

I looked around, but there was only Selene. It must have been her who spoke. When I touched her hand, it was cold.

Flashes of her memories were visible to me. It seemed as if her life was flashing by so quickly. It was as if I could see all the

164

happy and sad memories—betrayal, grief, peace, smiles. We fell together like one, crashing hard into the ground. However, I did not feel anything. Looking around, I realised we were in a place I had never seen before. Then I saw my father walking up to her and helping her up. I could not hear anything during this scene. It went by quickly, but it was when my father accepted the gift. "In exchange for the gift, your father had to make a promise." The ghostly voice, Selene, said.

I was no longer in Selene's memories but in the mini paradise room. Her eyes were fixed on me, and she appeared more alert. However, there was still a black liquid coming from her eyes. "What was it?" I asked.

Putting her hand on my upper forearm, she said, "We have been bonded since you were placed in your mother's womb. It is only you-" She went limb to limb in shock.

Someone grabbed me from behind, causing me to gasp.

40. Rame

As I was pulled from the closet, I gasped. Upon looking around, I noticed Sebastian.

"What were you doing in here?" He asked, pissed.

"What was Selene the Guardian doing in there?" I asked, getting up from the floor.

As he looked away, he said, "She came to me again. She stated that something was wrong and that she needed to heal. And she just-" He paused, he looked back up at me. "Tell no one. No one can know the truth about the Guardians."

"What truth?"

"That special mortal weapons can harm them."

"Someone did that to her?"

He nodded.

"Were they aware of who she was?"

He shook his head.

"What if her being away made her worse?"

He nodded and stated, "They turn to ash when they die, according to her. Unlike us, they would be reborn on earth, eventually remember who they are and then return to being a Guardian."

"So, what caused such severe damage to her? How does she heal?"

"I don't know," Sebastian replied. "The only thing she needed from me was a hiding place."

Sitting on the bed, I asked, "How long has she been here?"

"Too long. However, she asked if I would not bother her. You should do the same." He paused, "Stay in the other guest room." No one should be in this room but me."

I nodded, getting up. "What did you promise her?" I asked when I placed my hand on the door handle.

"My child that has the strength of a guardian. But I have failed in creating one." Sebastian said, looking at the closet doors.

I was enveloped in darkness, the same pressure caused by Dark Matter Magick. However, this time I was able to breathe. The voice of Ezra rang out, "Cleo…"

Sitting up quickly, I gasped. "Ezra?" I glanced around. I was still in the guest room. As I sighed, I placed my head in my hands. "It must have been a nightmare." I whispered to myself.

I am not ready to face Mortimer but prepared to return home. Since Selene touched my forearm, I have felt a tingling there. Is there anything I can do? The only difference between me is that I lose control of my powers. They start to control me instead of the other way around. Could I be the child with guardian powers? It is possible that Selene is simply tired of waiting.

I arose from bed and began to prepare for the day. Estrid

had prepared some clothing for me last night. She selected a cropped white tee with a tight-fitting spaghetti strap printed dress and Doc Martens for me to wear.

I left the room. As Theo left his room, he smiled gently at me. "Are you ready for the after-party?" Theo asked. "The party is only a few hours away."

I shrugged, "As good as I can be. Sebastian has tried to give me tips, but I still do not have the ability-" I paused for a moment.

He touched my shoulder and said, "You'll figure it out. Everyone believes in you."

With a quick smile, I turned to walk away.

When I entered the informal living room, Esme drank coffee and looked up at me. "Hello, Little Crow. How are you feeling?"

I shrugged, "I'm just ready to get Ezra so we can go home."

She didn't say anything, just nodded.

"Sebastian left, didn't he?" I asked.

She shook her head and said, "He has not left yet. He has never been down here before. He seemed upset that I allowed you into his room, and he did not want you in Elizabeth's room, either."

"I guess he is just territorial." I began going to the kitchen to get something to eat. I need as much energy as possible. I had only a few hours to prepare, but it took forever. Ultimately, I only had one chance to fight Mortimer, and I cannot go back and do it over.

Neither Theo nor I were permitted to go above ground, so we played board games or read books. Or simply staring up at the ceiling. Sebastian only trained with me a few times. However, he was quieter than before. Whenever I attempted to ask him more about Selene, he left the training room.

Sitting on the kitchen barstool, I began drinking blood from the glass. Also, I grabbed some dark chocolate.

Inhaling deeply, I took a deep breath. Many people depended on me, so I needed to be sure I had a guaranteed method of winning. It was not as if I could enhance my powers. I took a couple more sips.

Violet.

She is a doppelganger. The Blood Empowerment slipped my mind because I was so focused on Syphoning.

In a rush, I approached Esme and said, "Hey, can you do me a favour?"

43. Drapetomania

Esme's guards took some time to locate Violet, but they eventually did. She was brought here wearing a blindfold. She seemed terrified as we sat in the informal living room. Mainly when she maintained eye contact with me. Estrid, Theo, and Esme waited for Violet to calm down in the formal living room.

"You've changed." Violet stuttered, "You've been tempting fate, haven't you?"

I was confused as I looked at her, recalling the ghostly voice from Sebastian's old room. "What are you referring to?"

"You started tapping into your full potential." Violet said.

"Yes, but only because I need to get home." I replied, "I need to get home. I should not be here."

"So why did you bring me here? What do I have to do with you getting home?" Violet asked.

"I need your blood."

Violet tensed up in response.

"I would prefer if you did not say no, but you have a choice." I began, "I need to use your blood to enhance mine to defeat Mortimer."

It was clear Violet was shocked. "You will use your powers when you do not know how?"

170

As I nodded, I said, "Mortimer has the witch from that night and a hostage. It is game over if Mortimer manages to capture me or Theo. However, if I had additional power from your blood, I could defeat Mortimer and that witch."

"But what if they get you while you have the blood boost? Is Mortimer going to get stronger?"

I shook my head and said, "He shouldn't become any stronger than he was previously. You should be able to put him back as long as there is an heir."

"Then why do you need my blood? We have an heir, so you should not have to fight him."

"He has my mate. He intends to fight me to obtain the last bit of his soul from me and Theo. Because I do not have complete control over my powers, I will only need to hit him once if I use your blood boost. Then Lord Sebastian can absorb any power that I cannot control. I can go home with Ezra, and everything can return to normal."

"Okay. That's fine, but I won't be there. Let's get a vial of my blood so you can take it with you."

"I apologize for interrupting. A blood boost must come from the essence of the individual. Otherwise, the blood is simply blood." Esme replied, "Lady Cleo must take a drink directly from you for the blood to be effective."

Violet appeared to be afraid.

"Sorry, but you must be present for this plan to succeed." Esme replied, "I know you do not want to do that. Nevertheless, we must ensure that everything goes according to plan to protect the future.

"I don't want to be surrounded by vampires." Violet murmured.

"Why is that? It's not like-" Esme began.

"The Valentines are after her because of the blood she has." I realised as I spoke. "I am sorry, but I will find another solution. You are welcome to leave a vial of your blood. You can leave if you wish." I began to stand up.

Esme grabbed my arm and said, "Are you sure that's a good idea? Are you sure you can fight him in your current state?"

As I shrugged, I replied, "I am not sure. I hope that it will suffice."

Esme dropped her hand and asked, "But what about the future? Should you lose, then-"

"We simply need to discover who the heir is and have them as a backup plan in case things do not go as planned." I smiled softly at Violet, "I'll see you around."

I went to the guest room where I had been staying. I flopped on my back on the bed. I will not be able to stop Mortimer; I will lose control. Couldn't it have been someone else? I did not wish to live this life; I wanted to return to my human form. Casting the Human Spell on a pureblood more than once can cause significant damage to the pureblood. A pureblood can become a vampire of level F.

My arm was placed over my eyes as I sighed.

I hope Ezra is okay. I hope he is not suffering torture just because he happens to be my best friend.

42. Plaxondry

After getting ready, Esme gave me a dress to wear. This dress had spaghetti straps; the dress was tight under the boob and flowy on the rest of the body. The dress was made of navy silk with a thin black lace covering the breast and flowing down the remainder of the dress. Esme helped me with my updo and even wore one of her simple tiaras when she was my age.

In the formal living room, I waited for Theo to finish. As he did not want to wear a tuxedo, it took him some time to find something that he would wear. Theo wore a white blazer, a navy shirt, and blue denim jeans. As he spun around, he asked, "What do you think?"

I smiled softly, "Very nice."

"You look great too. I like the tiara." he said.

"It belongs to Esme. Since I did not get to wear something of hers while I was growing up, she wanted me to wear something of hers."

"That's sweet of her." He started walking up to me with his elbow out. "Are you ready?"

I nodded.

"Let's get this over with." I could hear his heart beating faster.

There was a large crowd at the party. There were species of every kind present. I remember going to these when I was younger, but I don't remember much since I always fell asleep after a few hours.

Several people were also in the gardens, which were much quieter than the ballroom. It was not classical music but music from the early 90s that was popular then. Typically, pop music goes classical. Mum likely changed it after some time.

As we entered, eyes turned towards us. The pureblood and the hunter linking arms. Hunters were not considered purebloods during this period. It was in the late 2000s that they first received the title of royalty or pureblood.

As I looked at Theo, I unlinked my arm. "Should we remain together or separate?"

"I think we should stay together." Theo started, "We both know Mortimer has that witch with him."

I nodded, "Okay," I pointed towards the more dense crowd, "Let's go check that area to get it out of the way."

When we began walking in that direction, I felt a hand grab my arm. "You shouldn't have come." A familiar voice said.

After seeing Ethelred, I turned to look for Theo, but I was no longer at the party. "Where-" I started.

"A small pocket world that will not last long." Ethelred said with panic in her voice, "You need to leave. You shouldn't have come."

Looking at her confusedly, I asked, "Aren't you the one

174

working with Mortimer?"

She nodded, "I had no choice. The sword he wields controls me, Winter Moon. He gave it to Ezra but has managed to maintain control over me." She explained, "I have seen the future, and Mortimer will defeat you. The wicked will win, as the future has already been changed."

"What do you mean about Ezra? So, Ezra is okay? How could Mortimer defeat me? As a pureblood vampire, I can control Dark Matter Magick."

As the witch sighed, she said, "Yes, but Ezra will be using Winter

Moon. The blade is embedded with shifter venom. Mortimer will use Ezra to fight you; that is how he will win."

"Ezra would not fight alongside Mortimer. Erza knows everything Mortimer did to me." I tried to push her off of me, but she was too strong for me to move.

She stated, "Once I let go, this world will collapse." But I continued to resist her grip when she said, "You are not going to listen to me. You are fighting fate," she declared. It was then that she let go of my grip.

When I fell backwards onto the floor, Theo was there to help me up. "Are you okay?"

My head nodded in agreement, "I think we may have a little problem here. Ezra is fighting alongside Mortimer and Ethelred for whatever reason." I brush off any dirt I may have picked up.

"What do you mean Ezra's fighting Mortimer? How do you know?" Theo asked, panicking.

"Ethelred created a pocket world and told me about it. I don't know whether this is true. At least we know they are all present, and we must remain vigilant."

175

Theo nodded as we made our way through the dense crowd. As neither of them appeared, I turned towards Theo. "I do not believe they are among this crowd. Let's take a look at another area of the ballroom."

Theo nodded, "Are we sure they're here? Ethelred made that pocket world, but I heard she was a powerful witch. Maybe they're not here?"

I shrugged, "Maybe they are not here, but where else could they be? Mortimer has said that he will be here."

After thinking for a moment, we both looked at one another and said, "The lake." We started rushing over there when a powerful force struck us and the people around us. Everyone fell to the ground.

"Princess, I warned you not to come." Ethelred said.

Suddenly, I felt something sharp at my throat. I looked up to see Ezra holding a sword to my throat. Winter Moon sword with shifter venom embedded in it. There was a stinging pain in my neck, "Ezra?"

As I looked behind him, I noticed Ethelred and Mortimer standing beside each other, Mortimer smiling and Ethelred looking sad. "Never expected your mate to be so easily brainwashed, but look at him! He does not care about you at all." Mortimer exclaimed.

Looking back at Ezra, I could not see anything in his eyes. I reached for him and said, "You've returned to me."

Ezra swung his sword at my hand and sliced it. After hissing in pain, I pulled my hand back before he attempted another attack. The ring he was supposed to wear to protect him was not on his finger.

"He is a perfect little soldier. I was not expecting him to be so skilled with the blade." Mortimer said, "Ezra, release the

Princess. We must travel to the lake."

Taking a few steps back, Ezra allowed me and Theo to stand up. When we looked at each other, I could tell he wanted me to try to use my powers, but I had no control over them. I shook my head.

"Cleo." I looked over to see Estrid throwing a sword at me. There was a sword that resembled Blood Fang. This blade was used to defend the Night Court. It is capable of absorbing both vampire venom and shifter venom. As a result, both stronger parties are adversely affected. If the two are mixed, the Fae may suffer harm. Due to hunters being mixed with all, they may also be harmed as a result.

My arm was sliced as I reached for the sword. Once again, Ezra swung the sword at me. He does not feel anything for me. Moreover, he was not wincing in pain due to his previous injuries. "Is it killing you as it is killing me, Ezra? Return to me." I pleaded with him. In response to the shocking pain caused by the sword, I gasped. I noticed the skin around my wounds was turning dark green. He looked at me with a cold expression as I looked back at him. It was as if he had become a completely different person. Was he not also affected by our bond?

Ezra attempted to take another swing at me, but I was able to dodge just in time. Tucking and rolling, I was able to pick up the Blood Fang. I could not control my powers until I was confident I could defeat Mortimer, Ezra, and Ethelred.

I prepared myself for the next attack that Ezra would make. I was familiar with his abilities, the energy balls. I do not intend to harm him but rather to knock him out.

There was another wave that knocked more people over. "No, Sebastian. It's her fight now." I looked back to see Esme,

Estrid, Sebastian and many others on the floor.

"My attention would be focused on the lover boy, Princess." Mortimer replied.

Looking back, I noticed that Ezra had attempted to use a jump attack against me. Using my sword, I managed to block it and force Ezra to fall. He held out his hand to gather an energy ball; I sliced his wrist before he could release it. As he gasped in pain, I kicked his blade towards Theo. "Theo, take it!"

Theo grabbed it just before Ethelred could use her powers to take it back. It almost appeared that she was relieved that she did not get it.

Is it possible that Mortimer has the power to control her?

"I was hoping you wouldn't be like this, Princess," Mortimer sighed. "I fear things will have to be taken up a notch." He held up a jewelled item that resembled an opal that sparkled. "Ethelred, it is time for plan B." I looked over at her; she looked horrified and shook her head. However, Mortimer had the jewel that controlled her, so she had no choice but to submit.

She began to sparkle just as the opal did, and she took a deep breath. A powerful explosion followed, knocking the remaining party members off their feet. The room was filled with a white fire that did not burn.

I jumped and searched for the sword as I lay on the floor. Theo did not possess the sword I gave him either. Behind me, I heard a scream and the sound of flesh being cut. I turned to see Esme staring at me, placing one hand at her heart as the blade was pulled back. I was splashed with blood. My eyes were filled with horror as I realised what had just occurred. As I collapsed to the ground, Esme fell towards me. Trying to assess the severity of her wound, I pushed her away a bit.

Suddenly, I felt a warm hand on the side of my face; it was her hands, "I'm glad I got to meet you, Little Crow." Esme whispered. A soft smile spread across her face.

As I shook my head, I replied, "No. I can't-"

Her body became limp in a moment, and a faint glow emanated from it as she slowly turned into glowing dust.

I heard Mortimer laughing and looked up to see he had Ezra in his grasp. "The blade gently sliced his neck. It would be best for you to follow me, Princess. Otherwise, your mate will suffer the same fate as your grandmother."

When I felt a hand on my shoulder, I looked up to see Theo, who nodded in agreement.

"You want us to go?!" I exclaimed; I could feel the tears falling down my cheek.

Theo nodded, "So, no one else shares the same fate as Lady Esme. The future cannot be changed."

I shook my head in disbelief, "If he wins, there will be more death. Do you think that's-"

Theo leaned towards me, whispering, "Violet."

As I looked past Mortimer's group, I saw her standing alone. Has she decided to help us in any way?

43. Eleutheromania

Yet another power wave hit everyone, but no one could get up this time. Only Mortimer, Ezra, Ethelred, Theo and I stood up. "It is your responsibility to ensure that no one leaves." Mortimer whispered into Ethelred's ear. It was barely audible to me.

The white fire was growing in size, but it was not causing any harm to anyone. When I glanced back at Sebastian and Estrid, they could not move from their position. Estrid was focused on the ground where Esme was last while Sebastian observed the fight. Looking back at Mortimer, he was smiling. "Well, come on. I am sure you already know where we are going."

Theo and I nodded as we followed Mortimer down to Crystal Blue Lake. To calm my breathing, I took a deep breath in. I was still wired up; I needed to figure out how to contact Violet. I would not want to, and if I had the choice, I would rather live away from all of this. We made our way through the Haunted Forest.

When I noticed someone was following us, I turned as little as possible so Mortimer would not see them. It was Violet.

I gently bumped into Theo and gestured to look behind us with my head. She smiled back at him as he waved gently at her. Taking our attention back to Mortimer, he had Ezra walk in front of him, saying, "If you try anything, Princess, I am going to kill the lover boy. He will walk straight into the blade if I ask him."

I turned my attention to Ezra. "When everything has been completed, will Ezra return to how he was?"

He snorted, "There is no reverse for this slave spell except death. After completing everything, I am sure I will kill him anyway. His only purpose is to trap you. Now that's over with," Mortimer shrugged, "he's completely useless."

My first thought was to launch at Mortimer, but I knew that would ruin whatever chance I had of getting us all out alive, or at least primarily alive.

I noticed that the lake is pretty close. There must be a way to get the jewel from Mortimer. That is what controls Ethelred. If I were to obtain that, would I be able to free her and put an end to Mortimer? Would she help us, or would she leave us?

I shook my head; no, Ezra remains under his control. Mortimer may have Ezra walk into the lake. There must be a way.

We arrived at the lake, where Mortimer broke free from his cage within my mind. While I was still a hunter/human, he and my hunter sister, Natalia, attempted to kill me, but I could stop them with my waking vampiric abilities.

"How ironic is it now, Celine," Mortimer said as he looked over the lake. "The free one will be me, while the one who defeats me will be trapped by duty. No matter how many losses I have suffered. It only takes this one time, this one victory!"

After pushing Ezra to the ground, he turned towards us. Ezra lay on his side, facing the lake. "Theo, since you were the first person I met." Mortimer gestured towards the lake.

Theo nodded, "I don't want to stand in the lake."

"You must. I can only regain my powers if I trade yours for mine."

In response to Theo's gaze, I nodded. I watched him step into the lake. Mortimer's grin grew, "I cannot wait to be whole. No one can understand what it is like not to be whole. An empty shell of what you once were. That witch, Celine, tried to obstruct my path and caused me pain."

Looking behind me, I attempted to locate Violet. Mortimer cast a spell as he began speaking an ancient language. As I felt a sharp pain run through my body, I watched as Theo fell to his knees in pain as well. Even though I am not in the water, the spell affects both of us.

I felt a sharp stabbing pain on my upper forearm as a whisper said, "Tempt fate." As the lake started to glow softly, it was difficult to see the glow through the Dark Energy the lake had accumulated over the years since Celine was there.

I don't know what tempt fate means.

I looked for Violet, who was nowhere to be found; I needed this to stop immediately. I felt my knees were giving out, but I knew that if I fell, there would be no way to get up again. It reminded me of the pressure I felt while training with Sebastian. Could this be Dark Matter from the lake? Is this Mortimer's full power?

My attention was drawn to Theo, who was violently coughing. Blood was coming from his ears, nose, mouth, and eyes. Similar to what happened to me, I do not have much time left.

As Mortimer continued the spell, an echo circled us.

As I muttered whatever strength was left, I hurried over to Violet. After slamming my teeth into her neck, I could see the face of the witch who created this Doppelganger, all its versions: the past, the present, and the future. Violet was fighting against me, but I was trapped in the vision of them. I could not find my way out of the maze of their lives. It was as if I had become all of them and lived their lives. When a hand touched my shoulder, I turned to see Esme. It was difficult for me to breathe.

"You must take a step back from everything you see. You are not truly living their lives, Little Crow. Come back before it's too late." Esme reached out to me, and I felt a tear run down my cheek. They lived such a simple life. It was tempting to stay. I reached for her hand, and then everything went dark. After taking a moment to blink, I was back in the forest again. I felt the warm liquid coming from my mouth and wiped to see the blood.

Violet.

When I looked down at her, she appeared to be very pale. I noticed that she was still breathing. I did not get a chance to check on her when I heard footsteps rushing towards me. I stepped aside just as Ezra swung his sword at me; his movements were slow. Upon making eye contact, he no longer had whites in his eyes; they were completely black.

Was he a level F vampire?

As he rushed toward me, I knocked him to the ground, saying, "Ezra, just stop." I held him down.

His eyes were filled with tears, "I can't-" He muttered, "I can't get back to you."

Putting my hand on his cheek and rubbing it with my thumb, I said, "I believe in you. You have the strength even to come this far. Stay here and let me finish this so we can go home." I placed a gentle kiss on his cheek.

Softly, he nodded.

I glanced back at Mortimer and Theo. Theo was lying face up in the lake, glowing more brightly than before. As Mortimer turned towards me, he was still speaking the spell. As the weight of the magic no longer affected me, I felt a surge of power running through my body. As if I were floating, I felt free.

I rushed towards Mortimer, but he hit me with a wave of Dark Matter which didn't affect me. Putting my hands together, I concentrated on forming a ball of Dark Matter.

After forcing the ball towards Mortimer, it barely phased him.

Laughing, he said, "Dark Matter Magick users cannot harm other Dark Matter Magick users. It is for this reason that your father used Celine."

After feeling a sharp pain through my rib cage, I gasped in pain as more venom entered my body. Looking back, I saw that it was Ezra with the sword. It was difficult for me to breathe.

"It seems the wicked have won." Mortimer said, softly. "Now, this should be a simple task."

As Mortimer returned to the lake, he recited the spell.

As Ezra pulled the sword back out, I gasped again and fell. As I looked at Violet, she was still not moving. Is she dead? Why hasn't she moved yet?

Ezra's arms went underneath me as he picked me up. His hold on me was too strong, and I was in too much pain to attempt to push him off. The sharp pain from the spell was beginning to return to me. I groaned in pain. With me in his arms, Ezra began to walk towards the lake as I looked up at him. "Please don't listen to him. You can come back; let's go home." I muttered. It was hard to speak.

As black liquid fell from his eyes, I rubbed his cheek to wipe them away. He walked us slowly into the water.

"You'll tempt fate, won't you?" A voice echoed.

44. Metanoia

The water beneath was shockingly bright. As Ezra's head was submerged, I looked up. I began to float out of his arms as he sank to the bottom. I tried to swim after him, but he could not withstand the poison of these waters, especially not after what had happened to him. I reached out to him one last time before he sank too low. Eventually, I could grab him and pull us both above the water.

He was cold to the touch. "Ezra?" I whispered to him. "Please wake up." I began shaking him.

"That will not work, Princess. Your lover is very much in the past tense." Mortimer said, "One less thing for me to worry about."

Looking up at Mortimer, his eyes were glowing purple. He had regained some of his powers, so he would be nearly unstoppable if I were to die.

Since the water around me was nearly transparent, that indicates that it is no longer poisonous, correct? Didn't the waters previously heal?

I cupped my hand, placing it in the clear waters. Drinking water from my hand, I was careful not to consume the water itself. As I put my lips on his, I hoped most of the water would reach him.

I screamed as someone grabbed my hair and pulled me from the water.

You know it won't work, don't you? Do you know how long these waters have been poisonous? Mortimer had lifted me out of the water.

I thrashed against his hold, attempting to return to Ezra before he went too deep.

"Let me go!" I screamed.

"Why? The poisonous waters will not work on the Knight Clan, so I must kill you in the only way I know how to kill a pureblood Knight Clan member." Mortimer began.

I felt a piercing sensation in my chest. The Blood Fang was through me as I looked down in shock. As he pulled out the sword, I was left breathless.

I was thrown back to land by him. He gently glided over towards me, leaning down. His face inches from mine, he touched my chin, "You will always be my favourite, Princess. You awoke a new life I thought I would never have." He looked at the sky, "You gave me a new start in life. All thanks to you, the last Crow Princess." He looked down at me while I was struggling to breathe. He tilted his head, "I guess I missed your heart. Having not picked up the sword in a while, please forgive me that I could not give you a quick death as we will do with your friends."

Taking a deep breath, I realised I needed every ounce of strength. When I looked deep within myself, I realised that my string was now black. Why had it changed? I pulled hard on it, using the dark matter to heal my wounds. Suddenly, I had much more power than I had ever experienced before.

He was shocked when my wounds started to heal, terrified even.

As I placed my hand on his neck, I saw flashes of memory. I made sure to pull him along with me. The moments with his friends, the misfits against the purebloods who had wronged them, were evident to me. The group showed kindness and gentleness to me; what a happy family this was. I pulled myself out of the memories but made sure Mortimer stayed in the memories.

He was in a daze while reliving the memories he had made with his makeshift family. I am glad one of us could have one last happy memory. "We could have been great friends dealing with Dark Matter Magick together. If only we had met on better terms." I whispered, a tear rolling down his cheek. My whole being was filled with the power I had felt before. As I gazed towards the lake, I realised I could have stopped this if I had allowed the Magick to take hold of me. I turned to Mortimer and said, "I believe I have a solution to free both of us. I may not be a Light Matter user, but I have a bond with a guardian."

I pulled him close as I sunk my teeth into his shoulder. The life left his body as I drained every last drop of his essence. He felt heavy against my weak state. An ethereal glow emanated from his body as he turned into a million stars. When something small dropped on my chest, I slowly picked it up. It was an opal.

"It is time for us to be free." I whispered. When I turned to Violet, I saw she was starting to move. I felt a weight lift from my chest. I am glad that I did not kill her. While looking at me horrified, she was also glancing at Theo. "I will stay here if you wish to grab Theo, and you two get some help."

I could hear her swallow, but she nodded and rushed to Theo as quickly as she could. She was tripping a couple of times.

I watched as she assisted Theo up the hill. I hope they will both be okay. Looking back at the lake, I said, "Let's see if Ezra is okay." I began to walk into the water. As a bright light emanated from the lake, I covered my eyes.

I felt a weight pulled from within, "You tempted fate, didn't you?" I heard a small voice say.

I was able to breathe again. I blinked a couple of times, letting my eyes adjust to the light. I was in Sebatian's old closet, lying under the bent-over figure who did not seem dead. As she gently patted my head, her hair was the softest purple I had ever seen. She spoke softly, "We are one again. You have been away for a long time."

Looking at her confusedly, I asked, "What are you talking about?"

"The heir is near." She whispered, and I noticed that her eyes were closed. She slowly started to open them; they were glowing red. "You are no longer of mortal flesh."

45. Present Day

Looking around, I realised I was still lying next to the lake. I could hear so many conversions occurring at once, and the flashing light surrounded me. The pressure on my chest felt almost like a pop, which caused me to sit up. When I placed my hand on my chest, I noticed that I was no longer bleeding. The venom was no longer present in my system. As I looked up at the moon, I saw it was red. I felt a presence next to me.

Looking over, I noticed glowing pale pink eyes. As a bright light of pink grew around the person, I leapt to my feet.

"Hardin, stop!" I screamed.

The glow disappeared, "Is it you?" A deep raspy voice asked.

As I nodded, my legs felt weak and shaky under me. "Yes, who else could it be? Where is everyone?"

"Everyone has gone into hiding. I thought-" His voice trembled.

"What is happening, Hardin?"

"What have you done in the past, Cleo?"

Then I shrugged, not wanting to tell him, "I do not know. But I stopped Mortimer... Oh, shit, I must get to my parents."

I hurriedly approached the old animal housing, but Hardin blocked my path. "They will not be there. Kolby found them."

The voice that said this wasn't Hardin's, but a female voice. I turned to see Thea. While she did not appear any older than when I first saw her, she did seem different from the first time I saw her.

I shook my head, "No, that can't be true."

She nodded, "Kolby found out after Mr Gair assisted Kolby in entering Cypress. Thankfully, that was all Kolby wanted."

"Is everyone else okay?" I asked, voice weak.

"For the most part." Thea said.

"You tempted fate, didn't you, Young Crow?" said a female voice behind me.

My attention was drawn to a woman dressed in all black, her face covered by a hood. She did not have the same presence as wonderers. There was a much stronger feeling toward her.

"Who are you?" I demanded.

"A reaper." She chuckled. I saw her movements and took a few steps away from her. I could see that she was annoyed as she grabbed my wrist. As the blood moon illuminated my upper right forearm, I noticed a dark outline of a crescent moon forming. Her grip was too tight for me to pull away.

"Who are you?" I whispered.

"Her assistance prevents Valentines from taking over the remaining three towns." Thea explained.

"What towns have they not taken over?" I asked.

"Woemi, Narsi, and Kilus." Thea said.

The new girl nodded and let me go. "You have a lot to explain."

"Explaining for what?"

"All the changes you have made in the past, and how your soul is bound to the goddess we thought had died." She paused, "Until now."

Zero. Gloaming

"I don't know. Selene told me that we have always been bonded." I said, pulling my hand away from her. "Ethelred." I replied, grasping the opal tightly.

"Yes, Master." Ethelred said, appearing beside me. Her age had increased slightly since I saw her.

I handed her the stone, "I want you to live a peaceful life, even if I can't."

Relief washed over her as she smiled, looking at the stone in her hands. "I am finally free. Thank you, Princess."

"Cleo. My name is Cleo. I am no princess." I said.

The new girl looked at me confusedly and said, "More has happened than I anticipated. Ethelred was never meant to be released."

I shrugged, "Well, she is now."

The girl raised her hand to snap, but nothing happened. It appeared that she and the others were confused. "Why isn't it working?"

I shrugged, "I took doppelganger's blood so things won't work on me while I have it in my system."

The girl was dumbfounded. She looked at Thea, "She had changed everything."

Thea was not amused, "What did you change, Cleo? How

could you even change it so easily?"

I shrugged, "It is probably because I have been able to unlock the full power of Dark Matter Magick. I mean, I healed myself from the Blood Fang."

"How could that be possible? No Dark Matter user could heal themselves from the sword." Hardin asked Thea.

"No, it is not." Thea replied.

"The truth is that it is." Looking back at the lake, I could not determine whether Ezra was still alive. I wish there were a way to tell. "Did Ezra ever come back?" I asked.

"Ezra?" Asked Thea.

"No, he did not return. We are hoping that he was just stuck in the past." Hardin answered.

"He is not stuck in the past. My people do not know where he is." she explained.

"Who exactly are your people? I have never heard of reapers before."

"We work directly under guardians to ensure that everything runs smoothly. However, you are not contributing to the solution." The girl informed me.

"I do not understand why you are here, however. If we can not even know about guardians, then I assume that we are not supposed to know about reapers. Then why are you here?" I asked, looking at her.

"The things that are happening right now are not supposed to occur. We needed a more hands-on approach to try to fix it." The girl said.

"What needs to be fixed?" I asked.

"The Valentines should be human, Kolby should not have your parents, Natalia should be dead, and Ezra should be here, but you are not. It was meant for you to die in the past."

"How can we resolve this?" I asked.

Taking a moment to think, the girl shook her head, "I am not sure. There may not be a way to resolve the issue to prevent further damage."

"So what would you like to stop with first?" I sighed.

The girl quickly replied, "We need you to tell us where Selene is. It all began when Selene disappeared into the Wishing Well. Everything should have gone according to plan if she had not done that."

"Why is it important where she is?" I asked.

The girl seemed annoyed, "I don't have to explain anything to one with mortal skin."

"I no longer possess a sense of moral flesh. Explain why you need to know." I replied coldly.

"What do you mean you do not possess mortal skin?"

"I told you I have control over the pure form of Dark Matter Magick."

"Because the bond between you and Selene was completed." She looked down with her hand on her temple and sighed, "That Guardian is always troublesome." The girl looked back at me and said, "Once all the Guardians have returned to the wishing realm, everything will return to normal, but if things continue on this path, everything will be destroyed. Selene's return will make everything easier to resolve."

"I cannot tell anyone. It is not safe for her to travel."

"What do you mean by that?"

"Someone harmed her."

"No one mortal can harm a guardian."

"The creature was not mortal. She was fleeing from something within the wishing realm." I replied.

Glossary

Blood Empowerment:
Blood Empowerment is when a supernatural uses another's blood to enhance their own abilities.

Blood Fang:
Blood Fang is a sword that is used to protect the courts. It harms each race as it has vampire venom and shifter venom embedded in it.

Dark Matter Magick:
Dark Matter Magick is the dark form of magick that was handed down to the races to control. Most don't have access to this form of magick.

Devil:
A devil are supernaturals that deal with death magick, mainly fae and rippers will practice this magick.

Light Matter Magick:
Light Matter Magick is the light form of magick that was handed down to the races to control. Most don't have access to this form of magick.

The Council:

The Council is a group of supernatural to rule over the races as a whole. Each races has two representatives to make sure everything is fair and balanced.

The Fae Court:
The Fae Courts are run by each species and trade out after 400 Earth days, corresponding to the seasons they control. Supernaturals use the Fae Courts as a form of their zodiac.

The Night Court:
The Night Court is run by either vampires or shifter, it is decided on who rules by trials called, the Night Trials.

The Night Trials:
The Night Trials are picked by the Council to pick the next ruler of The Night Court. Not one Trial would be the same.

The Council:
Definitions

The Wishing Realm:
The Wishing Realm is the realm where Guardians stay. Only the ones on the Council and Rippers know about this realm.

Winter Moon:
The Winter Moon sword isn't well known among supernatural, but it looks exactly like the Blood Fang sword, but it has a white opal gem that controls a powerful witch. Most think the sword is just a myth.

Wonderers:

Wonderers are supernatural beings who are being punished for a variety of crimes where death is not the appropriate punishment. Each robe colour represents the time they have to pay.

About the Author

Author of The Haunted Series Trilogy, L.N. White has been writing stories since she was very young. She started with poems in high school, but eventually returned to writing books. Her experiences in both forms of storytelling helped her create The Haunted Series. She currently lives in Oklahoma City with her boyfriend and two pets. In pursuit of her dream of becoming a published author, she now works part-time as both an author and freelance writer.

You can connect with me on:
❸ https://lnwhitewrite.weebly.com

Subscribe to my newsletter:

✉ https://docs.google.com/forms/d/e/1FAIpQLSd9QoaOCZu7drzft Tiv7zaH7pp3GCrQeEOVPKtCviAZ4XA/viewform

Also by L. N. White

The Hidden (Book 1 of The Haunted Series)
https://books2read.com/b/bONGL9
Cleo makes a deal with an ancient being, which has been the root of a family curse. The story is set on an island off the coast of Scotland, where Cleo enrolls at Cypress Institute to learn more about the curse. Throughout the story, Cleo must confront the ancestral curse that has been passed down her family for generations. The book features supernatural beings, including soul bonds, a deal with a devil, and ancestral curses. As Cleo Martin navigates through a new world filled with supernatural beings, she grapples with the emotional trauma that comes with this new life. This adds emotional depth to the story, emphasizing the strength of relationships and the lengths people will go to protect each other. The deal with the devil creates a complex element in the story, as Cleo must confront the consequences of her actions. The setting of the book on an island off the coast of Scotland adds to the eerie and atmospheric feel of the story, making it perfect for fans of spooky thrills and chills.

The Fall (Collection of Poems: Vol 1)
https://books2read.com/u/mZ0YjJ
Explore the depths of the human psyche with this collection of dark poetry. From hauntingly beautiful odes of melancholia to more intense explorations of the inner landscape, this book takes readers on a journey of powerful emotions, dark revelations, and deep introspection. With a wide range of poetic styles and topics, this book will transport you to a realm of beauty, pain, and understanding. Perfect for fans of dark literature, this book will provide a unique and powerful experience.

Milton Keynes UK
Ingram Content Group UK Ltd.
UKHW040905171123
432750UK00004B/300